THE TALE OF THE RED QUEEN
AND OTHER STORIES

LEGENDS FROM THE DARK DESIGN UNIVERSE

by
NEIL CAMPBELL, LM COOKE,
BONSART BOKEL, DUKE BOX,
and NILS NISSE VISSER

With a Warning by Professor Elemental

THE TALE OF THE RED QUEEN and other stories
ISBN Paperback: 978-1-9162342-4-6
Companion to THE DARK DESIGN album *TWELVE TALL TALES*
A CBS Green Man Publication
Cider Brandy Scribblers
Brighton, Sussex
England April 2020

Editor: Nils Visser
Cover design: Neil Campbell
Back cover image: Nico Time (CC-by-20)

DEDICATION

Here's to Ignatius Donnelly, H.G. Wells obviously, Rudyard Kipling, and Edgar Allan Poe. And here's to Andrew Lang, and Robert Louis Stevenson, and here's to Sir Arthur Conan Doyle. Here's to E.M. Forster, and Mary Shelley's monster, and here's a toast to Mark Twain. And here's to Samuel Morris, Edgar Rice Burroughs, and of course…Jules Verne.

(from *Haggard Rider* by The Dark Design)

CONTENTS

WARNING FROM PROFESSOR ELEMENTAL

Polite Notice: Please Stop Reading This Book.

To continue further than this sentence is not only irresponsible but could be dangerous for both yourself and the world around you.

Do not turn another page.

Do not look at the front cover.

Do not read this sentence.

Ah.

I see.

You haven't heeded my warning. It seems that you are in need of further explanation. Perhaps you feel like the rules don't apply to you. After all, you've read books before, possibly even terrifying tomes filled with mottled monsters and shifty ne'er-do-wells up to midnight mischief. Those stories didn't worry you or cause sleepness nights. Goodness no. A brave soul like yourself probably found those books to be nothing more than a vivid escape from the grey world around you. But those stories were not these stories and those books were not this book.

Imagine howling wind and the tang of warm ale in your tin mug, are you really prepared to hear the story of woman who has just entered the tavern? And as you reach the end of her story, why can you smell the sea so strongly, even from the comfort of your reading room?

How long would you be able to stare into your reflection of Pandora's mirror? And would you be happy with what you saw? Delighted? Disgusted? If it showed you a secret, what would you do to keep that secret safe?

Ever been transported into nostalgia by music? Then you might have an inkling what a former Queen of the Skies experiences – though in her case abstract nostalgia becomes all too real and troubles an already unsettled mind. Or minds? Just mind that you don't lose your own.

Are you really prepared to gasp for another breath as you are rocketed to unseen heights, to places unseen by the human eye? Perhaps you'll hear conversations that should never be heard or see things that you can never be unseen.

Let us pretend for a moment that you and you alone are the chosen one who can read all of these and so much more, to study the intricacies of The Dark Design and come away unscathed. That you and you alone are the one who can hold these stories like no other. In that case, are you prepared to take responsibility for them too?

Because once each story is read, it is yours. And if the Red Queen, or the Lions of Judah escape their stories- are you really ready to take them on? To stop them wreaking havoc? To prevent them from changing this world forever? The universe of The Dark Design maybe constructed with a clockwork heart, but there is muscle and sinew and stars in its workings too.

Still, perhaps this is meant to be. It might be destiny that you happened to pick this book up right at this moment in this place. It could be that you have no choice at all but to keep reading. You are part of The Dark Design too. The caretaker, the librarian, the witness.

But have a care. There may still be time. If you aren't sure. If you aren't ready. If you feel you still have the will to do so, you should stop reading now.

You can't say I didn't warn you.

Professor Elemental
The Library of Forbidden Books
March 2020

WHAT THE DEVIL IS THE DARK DESIGN?

Well since you asked… The Dark Design is a secret society of time travellers who share a common purpose, namely they all work for a man named Othniel Cope...

So, who the hell is Othniel Cope? Well, 'hell' is the relevant word here because the common purpose of The Dark Design is to assist Mr Cope in escaping Hell and eternal suffering…

What the Hell? Well quite, it's not just any hell we're talking about here, it's the Hell of Hells, the place where all bad gods go to pay for all their crimes, post eternity naturally — And it was here where Cope began his life and where he will eventually return to pay his debt, unless he can somehow cheat his destiny…

Pay for his life? Well you see Mr Cope knows his maker and he's no god, just a writer with a gift for character and — well to skip to the end, Othniel Cope simply decided he was too real to be fictitious and decided to make a go of it on his own…

How? Well that's one of the stories yet to come, but we can tell you that Mr Cope's creator, a talented author by the name of Alan Campbell, gave his creation a particular talent in his superb novella *Lye Street*, the prequel to his critically acclaimed steampunkesque debut novel *Scar Night*… In *Lye Street*, Campbell gave his character the gift of communicating with demons…and, well, Mr Cope took the idea and ran with it and made the deal of the century…millennium…eternity …infinity…

And if you can imagine what kind of demon could grant him not only life, but reality itself, then you can probably imagine how little Mr Cope wants to get to the end and pay his dues…

Cue then The Dark Design, a collection of extraordinary individuals, caught, collected and conducted by the erstwhile Mr Cope…

Once again, the stories will come in time, but we can tell you that Mr Cope has secured the services of following persons…

Mr Tom Bones – Sax, flute and Smokey Mountain banjo – An immortal grave digger, who legend says has been cursed to live long enough to bury the last other living thing…

Mr Herashibold Endeavour – Bass, guitars, vox – A Subsonicist and graduate of Thwaites Military Academy. What need could Cope have for a man who is caught between dimensions?

Drusilla De Silva – Sax, flute, guitar, vox – Pirate Queen – There are no records of Ms De Silva prior to the discovery of her now deceased sister Daphne but her subsequent adventures on the high seas are legendary.

Tin-Eyed Tink Tinkerton – Accordions, keys, synths, banjo, vox – Tink lost an eye during a near fatal knife fight with a ship's monkey. Fortunately, or perhaps not so, he was given a pair of tin eyes by the ship's captain by way of apology. The Captain said he got them from some weavers, and ever since Tink has been able to see into the future. Unfortunately, his vision is quickening at an exponential rate and before long he will witness the end of time… Is Cope hoping for clues?

Casanova Crowley – Ukulele, vox, guitar – Mr Crowley is the secret and abominable love child of the world's greatest spy and lover and the world's wickedest man… His purpose amongst The Dark Design is as yet unknown, but ladies should be warned he makes a noise that only women can hear and can unclasp a brassiere with his mind…

Professor Simkins – Robotics, contraptions, and production – The professor is the last surviving protagonist of the Noble Peace Prize Wars. This was a time in the near future where Time Travel was discovered which set in motion a catastrophic chain of events spurned on by the desire of the world's scientists to *go back* and *FIX* all that was wrong with the world, thus creating a tsunami of paradox which eventually tore the very space time continuum into little pieces… Fortunately Professor Simkins realised this would eventually happen and went back in time to the day before the machine was showcased at the world's fair, nicked it and the plans, and forced the scientists involved to watch top gear re-runs until they were capable of nothing more than casual racism and lusting over motor cars. He now possesses the universe's only functioning Time Machine… Fortunately for Mr Cope, he isn't as good at playing poker as he thinks…

Gordon Vader – Guitar, trumpet, tubitar, vox, – Quite how the gin-soaked card player and amateur voodoo magician even made it onto the crew of the Star Class Steamer *The Dark Design* is a mystery to most… Fortunately for Mr Cope, and indeed for Mr Vader, he is a quite good at cheating at poker…

Othniel Cope – Guitar, harp, baritone ukulele, vox – Thaumatage and one-time work of fiction, Mr Cope's agenda is still unclear, although it would be safe to say running from impending and unimaginable doom and suffering is pretty high on the list… It must be said that Gordon Vader and Mr Othniel Cope have never been recorded as being in the same room at the same time and bear a striking semblance to each other…

So, you maybe be wondering…What's the connection between Alan Campbell and The Dark Design? Or is this all simply fan fiction? Well here's the clever bit… The Dark Design is the brainchild of Neil Campbell, the younger brother of Alan and also a writer, and here's the clincher… He was also the person on whom the character Othniel Cope was based….

To the music… The Dark Design are a steam punk band like no other, because they are truly the first band to embrace the single common thread between all the steampunk movements – music, stories, writing.

All of the songs on the album *Twelve Tall Tales* tell stories; from the tragic allegory of a man who falls in love with a clockwork girl (*The Problem with a Clockwork Heart*) to a gruesome account of one man's life aboard the Devil's steam train (*The Iron Heart*), to a rousing swing sea shanty about the most fabulous steamer ever made (*The Ballad of The Southern Swell*)…a sailor's near death experience and the tale of a mermaid Queen (*Queen of The Sea*)…an homage to the great writers of the Victorian/Edwardian Times (*Haggard Rider*)…The true story of one of the universe's most infamous assassins (*Xandie Rae*)...a stark warning from an aging femme fatale, beautifully sung by Mishkin Fitzgerald on the album *Twelve Tall Tales* (*Wages of Sin*)...a love story that transcends time itself (*Hanging in the Gardens Of Babylon*), a long journey and the power of a prisoner (*The Tale of the Red Queen*), and of course a reinterpreted version of the tale which started it all (*Lye Street*).

This anthology is a companion to that album, with some of the stories told in the songs re-imagined, embellished, and/or expanded by a handful of scribblers entirely unafraid (or blissfully unaware) of the risks they run in scribbling these tales.

LM Cooke – Author of steampunk and fantasy fiction (amongst others: *The Automata Wars* and *Asylum Chronicles*), musician, historian, occasional producer of risqué sauce, and all-round good egg (other than when she's in a plain evil mood, which may or may not be influenced by the presence or absence of cheese).

Bonsart Bokel – Opinionated YouTuber, creator of the ongoing Steampunk Beginner's Guide documentary, Radio Retrofuture for Fallout and other series, the narrator of short stories, model, decor building, and recently started drawing. Sometimes he does other stuff as well.

Nils Nisse Visser – Author of contemporary and historical fantasy, as well as the brand-new Smugglepunk genre. Smugglepunk is based on Sussex smuggling lore with a bit of Steampunk thrown in for good measure. Visser boasts that he's the world's foremost Smugglepunk author and assures us that this remarkable accomplishment has nothing to do with his currently being the only author writing in this genre.

Duke Box – A host, a presenter, a master of ceremony, a thrower of parties, a compare, a rabble rouser, a raconteur, a filler in between acts, a parlour games inventor and instigator.

Neil Campbell – Honestly, I have no idea who this might be, other than that he's never been recorded in the same room and time as either Mr Vader or Mr Cope, and bears a striking resemblance to those two…

Enjoy the music, enjoy the stories, be wary of unsupervised Time Travel, and if all else fails: Run like Hell.

Kind regards,
Othniel Cope

LYRICS: THE BALLAD OF THE SOUTHERN SWELL

INTRO

Ladies and gentlemen, legends mostly have some place in history. We all know that once there really was a Santa Claus and despite evidence to the contrary, I can personally assure you that there really was an Elvis...I'd like to share such a legend with you all tonight...Where I'm from more people have heard the story of *The Southern Swell* than folks here have seen that posh twat chasing Fenton round Richmond Park...And this legend has a moral...Never play the Prince of Darkness at Poker...So, ladies and gentlemen please charge your glasses...

To the finest ship ever made: *The Southern Swell*!!!

SONG LYRICS

In all the worlds in all of time,
There never was a prettier ship than mine...
She was a hundred tonnes and a half mile long
And could turn on the edge of a ten-cent coin.
Made of brass and teak and gold,
Mahogany and tempered oak,
She smelled like roses and French champagne
She was faster than a racing train.

Ladies and gentlemen please charge your glass
To the fastest of the iron clads
Her name of course was *The Southern Swell*,

But I lost her playing cards with the devil himself...

She had a grand piano made of glass,
Chandeliers of polished brass.
One hundred men kept her afloat
While I drank with queens and I danced with popes.
Her Ballroom design by Kingdom Brunel,
Her doors hand painted by Coco Chanel,
Her figure head carved from the skull of a whale
That I caught with bare hands off the coast of Brazil.

Ladies and gentlemen please charge your glass
To the fastest of the iron clads
Her name of course was *The Southern Swell*,
But I lost her playing cards with the devil himself...

I miss her, I guess we all do,
She was made by the Wests
And they knew a thing or two
Not only was she pretty but by god she was fast,
She tore the blue ribband by a day-and-a-half.
She eclipsed the eclipse into New Orleans,
Hell, I bet she'd have taken fever dream,
She was simply renowned,
From Shanghai to New Amsterdam
She was famous, but when you're holding pocket aces,
Wel, you gotta put them down...

So, ladies and gentlemen.
Please raise a glass to the fastest of the iron clads,
Her name of course was *The Southern Swell*...
And now, she's the fastest ship in hell.

LYRICS: THE IRON HEART

INTRO

There are moments when the hurricane is just a gale, but when the shapes in the dark are only shapes...today of all days the damned are near, this is a tale to test the stoutest of hearts this is the tale of *The Iron Heart*...

SONG LYRICS

Twenty-five years ago,
We had fourteen feet of drifting snow,
Had a wife back in Tennessee, badly badly missing me...
Now, I had no way of getting back
So, I climbed out on the railroad tracks.
I suddenly saw a train all black
With a signal red, signal light
From nowhere, well I heard a voice it said...
"Get on boy you've got no choice...
Don't worry though we'll get you home,
It takes more than a landslide or drifting snow...
To stop *The Iron Heart*...

She looked like she was black as coal,
And ran upon men's souls
And a hundred tonnes of dynamite
Couldn't put a dent into her side...
And I was scared...
But I hadn't eaten in about a week
So climbed up her running plate...
But as I stepped into her cab

I knew there was no going back...
Twenty-five years to this day...
I'm still upon that fucking train
And nothing I can ever do will get me home again.

So I warn you girls, girls and boys
If late at night you hear an eerie noise
And you see a red light on the tracks
Just turn around and don't look back.
Never step aboard *The Iron Heart*
For she's the devil's train alright
Never step aboard *The Iron Heart*
Unless it's a trip to hell you want

Twenty-five years to this day...
I'm still upon that fucking train
And nothing I can ever do will get me home again.

She's stopped a few times in the last twenty-five years
But of the passengers I'm the last one still here
I'm not proud of what I've done,
But my will to survive is strong...
Yeah, I'm not proud of what I've done,
But my soul it will linger on
I'm not proud of what I've done
But a man needs to eat
Somehow, I hope she stops again real soon
Cause I'm down to the marrow in the last girl's bones...

Twenty-five years to this day...
I'm still upon that fucking train
And nothing I can ever do will get me home again.

DEAR FRIEND
BY DAPHNE DE SILVA

Dear Friend,

If you have found this letter, then the following facts are true. You are in terrible danger and I did not die in vain. Naturally these statements will conjure a flurry of questions in your mind and I will do my best to answer as many as I can.

I first became aware of The Dark Design in 1882 whilst working as an astronomer at the Greenwich Observatory. Of course, back then I had no name for the source of the mysterious signals that seemed to be emanating from the outer rim of the Solar System, but within a day of deciphering the first message my troubles began.

There is too much to say here so forgive me if I skirt the details, but it was over a hundred years later in not only a new century, but indeed a new millennium where I would first set eyes on Mr Othniel Cope, vagabond and one time fictitious leader of the Secret Society and musical troupe I have come to know as The Dark Design.

It became clear shortly after our first meeting that Mr Cope himself was not the cause of the anxiety and apprehension I felt during each rendezvous...Indeed, I found Mr Cope an amiable and capable host and his erstwhile crew hold him in high regard for the most part. But I sense a steeper slope to his stories, and I couldn't escape the fact he was hiding something, and something astonishing.

Oh, brutal triumph, I was correct, but my accuracy brings me no solace for now that I finally understand the nature of those pursuing Mr Cope I realise that I too am in their sights. From what I have seen of their powers and methods, I can only pray for a quick death.

Mr Cope offered me protection, indeed he thrust it upon me and for all my foolish pride I resisted. I mean what chance do a Thaumatage, a card shark, a voodoo priest, a subsonicist, a pirate queen, a time spy, an automaton engineer and a scientist have against the Devil of all Hells. The being who presides over the Hell of Hell where after the eternity even the likes of Lucifer, Khali and Sett will one day be sent for judgement?

How in existence Cope got tangled up with such a monster is the square root of The Dark Design…

Nothing is perfect, a few days on the Telescopes at Greenwich and I could tell you that. Orbits shift, gravities fail, and things that were as clear as the nose on my face a moment ago, just plain aren't there a few hours later. When Dr Cartwright, my mentor and long-term family friend told me time was flawed too, I had no problems in believing him, although believing and conceiving are two different strokes indeed.

Now the problems with paradoxes are fundamental. They are quite simply infinite or then again maybe they aren't. Just to be safe I can confidently say that there is a paradox out there where paradoxes are infinite and another where they aren't. Confused? Well hold on to your braces because I've only just started. In another corner of a seldom tread paradox there is no doubt another Daphne De Silva who is blissfully unaware of Mr Othniel Cope , The Dark Design and all the shenanigans that accompany them and whilst she may live a long and content life, would this Daphne De Silva trade places with her? Not on your nelly and not for all the rings of Saturn and you simply have so see them close up. The feel of the coarse shingle between your toes as one takes a moonlight stroll along them is just one of the reasons I wouldn't change a thing, not that you can of course. I mean traversing time is one thing, changing it…well that's impossible. That said, if I've learned anything from my time with The Dark Design, I have learned that doing impossible things is Mr Cope's specialty.

Now, as I said, you have clearly become aware of The Dark Design and therefore I should warn you that strange events may follow. Should you begin to see shadowy figures on the periphery then fear not for the Dark Design will be with you, you can contact the notorious Mr Othniel Cope.

And don't worry about me, I've been through some tumbles in my life and being dead is the least of them.

I will write more when I can.

Meanwhile be safe…
Kind regards,

Daphne De Silva

TOM BONES TALE

Tom Bones was a gravedigger, not the most cheerful profession, but as he always said:
The dead don't bury themselves
Just one more today, the Gypsy Queen's husband. She said to have him buried afore midnight. Plenty of time left,.

But fickle mistress Fate had other plans in the shape of the Widow Hillary Robinson.
Tom, will you stay a while? It's been a year and I don't want to be alone tonight.
What's the harm? My latest corpse may be a Gypsy King…but dead's dead.
Tom chose the living over the dead…but despite Widow Robinson's ample charms it would be a decision he would come to regret…
UNBELIEVABLE!

Consoling Widow Robinson kept Tom busy until dawn. The Gypsy Queen was furious.
How dare you leave my husband to rot in the open air?
You promised me a burial and a burial will be mine
By the Devil of all Hell this I swear…
…When the last living thing dies, Tom…you will be there to bury its corpse
CHILLING!!
EERIE!

CURSED FOR ETERNITY!!
So…I am doomed…cursed by a Gypsy Queen to live forever…maybe I'll call on that Mr Cope after all.
THE DARK DESIGN
THE END

WHO'S COUP
BY NEIL CAMPBELL

I first met Professor Simpkin Nobel in an alternative Stockholm and I knew there was something otherworldly about the man. After a few hands of cards, brandy, some delicate questioning, and a sneaky look through Tink's tin eye and I was able to discern a little of the man.

His is a tale that will take time to tell. I can't explain everything, but I can tell you that he is the sole surviving nominee of the notorious Nobel Peace Prize War and the only man in history to have successfully altered time…

His story is a difficult one to tell, as it hasn't happened yet, and indeed it may never get a chance to happen. It's partly from him, it's partly from me, it's past tense, but hasn't happened yet and there are definitely bits missing/ made up… It took a full bottle of Brandy, but this is what he told me:

'In the year 2210 the world's scientific community came together for the first time ever, under the banner of the Nobel Peace Prize. We began a joint project to unite the human race in one single purpose…. The creation of a Time Machine…

'On June 22nd 2210, during its first manned trial, the machine travelled forward in time two years. I was the pilot. To this day I can't really explain what I saw or what I learned from that brief journey, I was only away for a few minutes. When I returned from the first ever journey in time I was terrified and quite literally unable to speak. A fellow scientist handed me an I-pen and before you can say Armageddon I had written something. It took me a moment to register that I had moved at all, but then I looked down and read…'

Hell On Earth

'We'd destroyed our world. Through our best intentions and our hardest work we'd ruined the planet. It was the paradoxes. I think that's why I couldn't focus on any of it. We'd built a time machine and over the next few years we'd gone back and changed everything that was wrong.

'We'd begun nobly, we saved species from extinction, overturned famines and averted disasters, but then we got sentimental and even vain; we'd spared great artists and even cultures. Soon we became judgemental, we demonised historical figures and executed en masse, we reversed the outcomes of wars and even started some of our own. Finally, we got just plain greedy… We stole land and mineral deposits, changed governments and all for a quick buck. I was only there for a second but I knew what I had to do. While they let me relax on a day bed in the lab I formulated my plan.

'They wouldn't listen, these were men and women of science, they were just far too bloody clever for that. So, while they analysed the data, I did what any sane person would have done, I built a bomb. The project was so secure that the research centre at CERN contained not only the machine, but all the research material.

'Building the device was easy, the time machine was so blindly important that the facility wanted for nothing. It took me two hours to kill my colleagues and save the world.

'I am a thief and murderer, Mr Cope. I executed two hundred of the best minds in history. I stole their blasted machine and in doing so I saved the world… or at least saved it for a while. They will remake this machine, Mr Cope, and when they do they will do the same thing… If we have learned anything about human nature it's that it's resilient.'

THE END

LYRICS: THE PROBLEM WITH THE CLOCKWORK HEART

INTRO

Perfection… That was simply the only way to put it…Cope stared long and hard into her eyes and took a moment to measure the gait of her arms again…Perfect…Cope trimmed a rogue hair with his razor and fussed over a thread on her gown…Perfect he thought for a third time…and replaced the calico cover…For the rest of the day he daydreamed through her construction, the plan had been perfect…his workmanship faultless…tried a thousand times to spoil her design and creation and could do neither…Perfect he thought to himself a final time as he removed the calico cover and stuck the key hard into her back…He wound the mechanism with a surgeon's care and on the hundredth stroke he released the key and as he did so he thought he heard something jar…

SONG LYRICS

When I first met you,
You were made of spring,
Bouncing around on everything,
I honestly thought you could last forever,
And nothing would ever slow you down,
After a while the rust set in,
And I realised maybe you were made of Tin

The Problem with a Clock Work Heart...
Is the End, it's not the Start,
All you get is a long long loose spring,
And pretty soon you can feel nothing...

You wound me up like a little robot
I couldn't stop drumming if I tried
And every time I looked at you
You nearly always cried
It got so bad in the end
You could hardly open your eyes

I'd pretty much do anything
To hear your clockwork heart tick again
But I know that I'm too late...
But take some comfort in knowing that
While clockwork hearts often stop
Seldom do they break.

LYRICS: QUEEN OF THE SEA

INTRO

Sailors who have tasted the sea and swam near death often tell tales of mermaids but it's said that only the drowned truly see them.

SONG LYRICS

Thirty years at sea
It was the worst storm there has ever been
We strayed too near the breach
And our lives would pay the toll
As I was tossed around
Took a breath and prepared to drown
I swear the rest was just a dream
But I swear I saw the most beautiful thing
It was the Queen of the Sea who saved me
She took me under the waves to safety
And in her palace by the edge of the sea
We drank wine and danced all night
Under bioluminescent light
But in the morning she said
"Gentlemen never spend the night."
I woke the next day back in the raging surf
Clinging to a barrel for all that I was worth
I was pulled from the sea
By the tallest girl I had ever, ever seen

Collapsed upon the deck and swam for days
In fever dreams...on the *Rose of the Sea*,
I tried to tell them where I'd been
Captain Hannah smiled and laughed and assured me
That the worse had passed
She told me to take myself to bed,
But she whispered something as she did...
It wasn't a dream she said,
But a mermaid I'd seen,
It was...but but ever since that day,
A little thought'so been nag nagging away...
What if I didn't make it out
And to be fair I've had my doubts
But that could only mean...
The whole thing's just some recurring dream
And the truth is I died beneath the waves...
And the Queen of the Sea who saved me
Was just a trick as the oxygen leaves me
And I'm drowning and I always will be...
No Queen of the Sea to save me
Just a trick of the light as my life leaves me,
But if I am going out, I'll go out in my own way...
With the Queen of the Sea who saved me,
She'll take me under the waves to safety
And in her palace by the edge of the sea
We'll drink wine and dance all night
Under bioluminescent light
And in the morning, she'll turn to me
And tell me everything is alright...

LM Cooke
SALT

SALT
BY LM COOKE

The beer tasted salty. The man at the bar wiped foam from his upper lip, set down the empty tankard with a clatter and gestured to the innkeep. 'Another!'

His is a tale that will take time to tell.

His story is a difficult one to tell, as it hasn't happened yet, and indeed it may never get a chance to happen.

Another foaming tankard was set in front of him. He fumbled in his pocket for coin, but the innkeep waved his money away. He couldn't remember what he'd paid for the last round, if he'd paid for the last round. It was of no matter. He took a gulp from the fresh tankard. Still salty. Perhaps it was the sea air. Or perhaps the ale was off. That might explain why the innkeep was giving it away.

A flicker of movement across the room attracted his attention. He looked up from the ale. Eyes, the strangest eyes he had ever seen, met his own. Those eyes almost glowed, bioluminescent in the murk of the bar. Then, in a blink, they were gone. He was left with an impression of a woman, like an afterburn on his retinas. She was wildly incongruous in this dimly lit, crowded place. He wondered why she was here. He wondered why she was not causing more of a stir among the inn's regulars. Not one man raised his face from his drink, not one man so much as even glanced knowingly at his neighbour. Their faces remained shadowed. He would not recognise any of them, he realised, if he should pass them on the street.

Outside the rain lashed at the windows. The building creaked and rocked in the wind, like a ship out at sea rather than a landlocked structure. The roof leaked, and water trickled steadily through on to the floor. The innkeep made no attempt to catch the drops; the wooden floor was awash. The fire in the hearth guttered, battling both the damp and the wind to stay alight. It gave out little enough warmth as it was. The entire building was cold, the rain-damp air clammy. He shivered. Took another gulp of foamy, salty beer and turned to survey the back of the room.

She was there. Pale, so pale, her hair foaming down her back, and her eyes, those eyes he had first glimpsed a moment ago, like cold blue fire. She was luminous in the dark of the inn. It was impossible to conceive how the men around her did not notice her incandescence. But they didn't. Every one of them kept their eyes glued firmly on their drinks, heads down, faces concealed by the gloom.

He blinked and she was gone once more. Perplexed, he rubbed at his eyes. They were bleary and smeared with salt; his eyes stung. When he blinked again, there was not even the space where she might have stood. The faceless drinkers had closed ranks as if she had never been there.

A hand, more chill than the air in the room, rested briefly on his shoulder. He started, almost spilling his drink. Her hand was slender, long fingers, the wrist delicate. Once again, its pallor was startling in the dark of the room, against the blue of the rough fabric of his shirt. He was wet through from the persistent damp, he realised for the first time, the fabric clinging to him soddenly. Her hand was ice.

'Who? What?' He turned, looked into those cold-fire eyes. They held his gaze. He had stared into these eyes before, he realised, and not only when he had seen her across the room earlier. They were too familiar, too knowing. Yet he could not recall ever having seen her before this day, and a woman like this he would remember. A woman like this, anyone would remember. She was slim, willowy. Every line of her body was fluid, flowing from one movement to the next. Her hand slid down his arm, drew him to his feet. This, too, was familiar. She had drawn him up before somewhere, somehow, with her slim, dangerous fingers on his arm. Her grip would be strong, far stronger than it should be for a woman of her stature. Standing, he towered over her, but he knew without knowing how that she was far stronger than he.

Her eyes burned cold like the depths of the ocean. He tasted salt on his lips, from the rain, from the beer, from the incessant damp in the air. She was speaking, but he couldn't make out the words, the sound was muted, lost in the cold, dank air of the inn, could not penetrate the thickness of the atmosphere.

His legs felt weak, alien; they could not support him. Her hand on his shoulder was heavy, weighing him back down to his seat; he went down easily. She was still speaking, he realised. But not to him. She was addressing the room at large. They did not look up, but the entire inn was silent, waiting on the words of this one, strange woman.

And now he could hear what she was saying. Her words rippled like the waves on the shore.

'The first time I saw him, he was a child', she said.

'His parents brought him down to the beach. He played in the sand with a cheap bucket and a spade, constructing a gigantic fortification around himself. Each castle wall was painstakingly rendered. He decorated the ramparts with shells. He wrote his name in the sand next to the giant castle, an author signing his work.

'Connor was his name.'

The woman paused her telling, stepping away from him to survey the room. Left on the bar stool, he frowned. That name – Connor – sounded familiar. Had he known someone by that name? What was his own name? He could not quite recall. The beer… the room swam before his eyes as he rubbed at them, the salt stinging. But the woman was continuing, and despite himself, he felt drawn to listen to her unearthly voice.

'Even then, as a cherub-faced boy with a shock of brown, curling hair, I could see the interest in his eyes as he gazed at me. His eyes were so blue they could have been of the sea. They did not waver as the first of the waves collapsed his castle of sand. I knew that one day he would be my lover.

'As he grew, so did his interest in me. Time and again I saw him on the beach, first with bucket and spade on the sand before progressing to games in the water, paddling and splashing, jumping over the foamy waves. At last he ventured properly into the water to swim in the shallows near the beach. At other times, he would walk down the narrow piers to gaze into the waters swirling beneath, and to sit and swing his legs in the sea breeze. Or he would climb the cliff paths and peer out across the horizon. Each time I looked at him, his sea-blue eyes returned my gaze a little more intently.

'One day, grown to a young adult, he came to me. In a small, wooden boat, the first he ever owned, he left the safe, shallow waters of the beach and rowed out past the protection of the headland, into the deep waters of the open sea. The effort left his arms a-quiver with exhaustion and his back stiff and sore. The sweat that dried on his body was like the salt of the sea. That night I rocked him in my arms as he lay back in his little boat. That night, the love in his eyes as he gazed at my rolling blue waves and gentle lapping waters, was unmistakeable.

'As he grew older, he forsook the land and took up as a fisherman. First, he served in another man's crew and though the captain did not love me as Connor did, still I spoiled that boat with the fish that I guided into their nets. Their hauls were bountiful and their pay bonuses great, so that each crew member was able to buy their own fishing boat. Each thanked his god for his wonderful luck. Each cursed his god when his luck turned, and his catches dropped, and before long, each had sold his ship and once again crewed for other captains. I focused my attention on Connor's vessel alone, and he continued to enjoy wondrous hauls on every voyage. My reward was the eternal love in his eyes as he stood in the prow of his ship and gazed out into my swelling depths.

'One day, he brought a woman out to the deeper waters, using the little rowboat that he still kept for sentiment's sake. The woman's hair was long and dark, and her laughter care-free. Her eyes were as mud brown as the land from which she came. Her wrists and ankles were slim and graceful, but her belly was swollen with child. Connor's child. He spoke to her with words of great tenderness, was solicitous to her every movement. That look in his eyes he had formerly reserved for me alone. A mistress, then. A rival for my affections. I looked hard at the laughing, brown-haired, brown-eyed woman. She was no rival. She was no challenge. I rose in a blue wave that swelled greater than her distended belly. I rose over the low side of the small rowboat, engulfed both her and her gargantuan midriff and swept them overboard. I held her tight to me as I drew her under and far away. The mass in her stomach weighed her down, dragged her to the bottom as I abandoned her. Her brown eyes gazed sightlessly upwards, her trailing fingers pointing at the sun in the sky so far above.'

The woman fell silent again. He wiped at his eyes. There was moisture there, like a tear, more likely a drip of rain. Something about this story seemed familiar. But he could not have heard it before. Outside, the storm was growing in force. The floor of the inn was awash with water. The lights flickered strangely, luminously. But the woman paid no heed to any of it. She was barefoot, he saw, but the chill water did not seem to discomfort her. The air in the room felt thick with damp, and the bar counter where he gripped it was slimy and spongy beneath his fingers.

The woman moved gracefully around the room, away from the fire that now burned a strange, cold blue. The other residents of the bar remained with their heads bowed, as if in worship, as she took up her strange tale once more.

'I left Connor sitting in the rowboat, untouched by even a droplet of water. He searched for his woman frantically. He dove until his breath heaved in his chest and he began to choke on the water he inhaled. I ushered him to the surface in a cloud of bubbles and forced him up over the side of the boat with an insistent wave. He lay on his back, choking and gasping. The saltwater that ran from his eyes mingled with that on his body so that the two were indistinguishable. Later, after he had returned to shore and raised the alarm, the great fishing ships set sail, searching, pouring light down toward my darkest places, places they could never hope to reach.

'No one ever found the woman. I held her close, picking at her soft tissues with gentle, insistent, watery fingers, feeding scraps of her flesh to my favourite fish. I ground away those brown eyes and trailing fingers until nothing was left to line my seabed but a cage of bare bones imprisoning a tiny, cartilaginous skeleton.'

The man on the bar stool frowned. Could he remember a woman – a woman lost at sea? But the brief image of a brown-eyed woman was rapidly supplanted by the reality of this other woman and her strange, luminous eyes who stood here now, telling her tale of the sea. No one else could compare to this ethereal creature, this concentration of sheer, of sheer...

Sheer what? He did not know. Could not focus. The air in the room was hard to breathe, it hurt his chest, his lungs. The water was cold, lapping at his ankles. The fire - how did it even burn now? – was bluely bioluminescent. And the woman spoke on.

'Connor tried to stay away from me. I did not see him on the beach nor on the cliff paths nor in his fishing boat nor anywhere near my waters. But I was not concerned. I knew the depths of his feelings for me. And soon after, he returned to me. Like an addict, he could not keep away. The tears on his face tasted of salt, proof positive if any was needed that he was part of me, as he had ever and always would be. In his little rowboat, as close to my waters as he could get without actually being within me, he railed and he wailed against the world. I rocked him, calmed him, soothed him on my breast.

"Why?" he asked me over and over. "Why?" I remained silent, but for the gentle lapping of my waves against the sides of his little boat.

'At length, he returned to the shore, and took up his old life as a fisherman. The mud-eyed woman was forgotten as he took to his trade with grim determination. I helped him, of course, and filled his nets full, but even I cannot account for the greed of man. They wanted more. They always wanted more. And so, even on a night when the worst of storms raged all around, still the fishermen sailed their boats and dragged their nets.

'I control much. I control the waves, and I control the water, my domain, but the air above, the lightening and the thunder, is beyond me.

'The boats shuddered under the assault of the waves and the wind. I let them fall. Connor's boat I watched, and Connor's boat I shielded as best I could from the onslaught. But I could not shield it from the lightning. It struck the mast, spread quickly to a barrel of pitch, and the boat caught fast aflame. Though I dowsed the fire, the ship was beyond repair.'

The inn fire, blue and cold, flickered. The lights overhead pulsed a similar colour. In the distance, Connor – was that his name? – thought he could hear music. His feet twitched uncomfortably, as if they wanted to dance but did not know how. As if he would fall if he tried to stand. As if they were not his feet, not his legs at all. The rising water was cold against his thighs. His fellow drinkers looked strange, their faces distorted, mouths open like fish gasping for breath. Only the woman was real, distinct, unearthly. Her strange eyes transfixed him. Her words fell into the heavy air of the inn like bubbles.

'Connor and his men slipped into my waters. His body felt light and frail as I cradled him against me; almost insubstantial.

His arms, having fought the storm for hours, had barely the strength to hold him up in the water.

'I could support him. I could return him to the shore.

'But he was mine, now, come to me at last, and I did not wish to let him go.

'I swept my waters around him, swirled him beneath the surface, to the magical centre of me, the place where I have no limits and am mistress of all. His eyes and mouth filled with my salt and he did not see or hear me as his lungs began to labour under the pressure. With my currents I squeezed and compressed, prised and coerced. His legs I held tightly, bound them together, while his feet I flattened and extended. The tail I created would serve him far better than those redundant limbs, now that he would be with me for all time. I forced my watery fingers into the flesh of his back above his lungs and sliced in gills like those of the fish so that he could breathe the air in my water and would never need to return to the surface again. Though he screamed and thrashed as I worked, and the look in his eyes was horrified, I knew it was for his own good and I did not release him until the work was done.

'At last Connor was finished. But the creature that swam from my fingers was Connor no more. With the tail and gills of a fish and the arms, chest, and horror-struck eyes of a man, he was unique in all the ocean. Despite all the legends that men had told on the shores, nothing like this had ever swum the seas before. As a merman he could swim with me and live in me for as long as he drew oxygen through his gills.

'We lived together. His blue eyes, as blue as the sea he now lived in, watched the keels of ships passing overhead. At first, he tried to follow these boats and attract their attention.

But the salt of my waters rusted his vocal cords and he found that he could no longer reproduce the speech of the land. The nets that trailed from the ships became a hazard and, frightened, he began to steer clear of the fishing boats. At length he became accustomed to being alone in me and his blue eyes lost that element of panic that had first accompanied his change. In time he began dreaming, and he dreamed a dream that comforted him. A dream of a storm, and a fishwoman who saved him from the sea. A dream of plain living, of beer, of the land.

'But his dream did not interest me. And I grew bored. There was a pretty pirate in Barbados with black hair and a golden earring and he looked at me with as much love in his wicked black eyes as Connor ever had with his sea-blue ones. So, I left Connor alone.

'Sometimes, when I remember, I visit. Sometimes I tell him that his dreams are only dreams, and that reality is far stranger than it seems he can comprehend. But he does not listen, just keeps on dreaming.'

The man at the bar blinked. He thought he had seen someone a minute ago, a woman, a beautiful, impossible woman, glowing bioluminescent. But no, he was imagining things. There was no one there, just the regular drinkers, just the fire crackling warmly in the hearth.

He took a sip of his beer, grimaced.

It tasted of salt.

THE END

ABOUT THE AUTHOR

LM Cooke is the author of 'The Automata Wars', a steampunk trilogy. Volume I, The Home Front, and volume II, The Front Line are currently available. Volume III, Back to Front will be released in 2020. She has also contributed to the various anthologies, including first three volumes of the steampunk compilations 'The Asylum Chronicles'.

LM Cooke is also a singer/composer and performer, currently performing as a solo artist. Her sound is dark with overtones of folk horror and a penchant for making things rhyme that really, really shouldn't. Her first album, Nursery Rhymes for the Apocalypse, is available from lmcooke.bandcamp.com/. She hosts a monthly musical podcast called The Murder Hour at mixcloud.com/lm-cooke/. She is an historian, a tarot card reader and a seeker-of-adventures who frequently finds herself followed by megalithic structures in a not-entirely-wholesome way. In her spare time she plots galactic domination.

She is available for book readings, presentations, workshops and musical performances – more details at LMCooke.com

"...transcends genre limits to such an extent that if we didn't call it Steampunk we'd have to call it something like Gothic-Science fiction-Crime-Thriller-Horror."

The Last Line Publishing House on 'The Home Front'
LMCooke.com

facebook.com/LMCookemusic/
lmcooke.bandcamp.com/
mixcloud.com/lm-cooke/

LYRICS: HAGGARD RIDER

INTRO

Plato said, "Books give a soul to the universe, wings to the mind, flight to the imagination, and life to everything." What does that imply about the authors writing those books? Within the realm of their story worlds they have godlike powers, inducing their readers to vivid hallucinations and subjecting their characters to woe as the plot unfurls. There is magic in their ability to speak to us long after they are dead, running riot in our heads...

SONG LYRICS

In the black hole of Calcutta, I met a haggard rider
He said, brandy sir, for I've a tale to tell.
I said, go on, but please don't take too long
For I've a dozen different matters to attend.
He said, cancel them at once, sir
For my tale is one of wonder
And you simply won't believe where it ends.
So, over a bottle of Courvoisier
He sated my curiosity, and this is what he said...

He said, I am the storyteller, one of those writer fellows,
I'll keep you guessing till the end.
He put our protagonist through ever mounting tragedies
Till they emerged victorious, killed the baddie, got the girl.

In the wilds of Ireland, I met a man named Oscar
He said come up to my attic

You simply must see this picture, I say
I said calm down I might pop round
After I finish off this lovely bottle of gin
He said don't mind if I do and while you pour me one too,
I'll tell you exactly how this sordid tale began
So over bottle of Hendricks
We went from foreword to appendix
And this is what he said...

He said, I am the storyteller, one of those writer fellows,
Keep you guessing till the end.
He put our protagonist through ever mounting tragedies
Till they emerged victorious, killed the baddie, got the girl.

Now at this point of the song
It's my duty to inform you
We couldn't possibly fit everybody in
But rather than leave them out
We thought would give them all a shout
And if we forget anyone please do write in.

Here's to Ignatius Donnelly, HG Wells obviously,
Rudyard Kipling and Edgar Alan Poe
Here's to Alain Lang, Robert Louis Stevenson
And here's to Sir Arthur Conan Doyle
Here's to EM Forster and Mary Shelley 's monster
And here's a toast to Mark Twain
Here's to Samuel Morris, Edgar Rice Burroughs
And of course, there's one chap that we left out.

On the steps of Notre Dame
Is where I met Jules Verne

He said, Écoutez-moi parce que J'ai une idée fantastique...
I said, sorry friend, je ne pas comprehend,
English please if you want to parley avec me.
He said, you British swine
Absinth will open up your mind
And who know what crazy worlds we'll find
So, over a bottle of butterfly,
He let my imagination fly
And this is what he said...

He said, I am the storyteller, one of those writer fellows,
Keep you guessing till the end.
He put our protagonist through ever mounting tragedies
Till they emerged victorious, killed the baddie, get the girl.
And save the world.

LYRICS: HANGING IN THE GARDENS OF BABYLON

INTRO

Cope looked again at the Journal...the equation tangoed across the page...it seemed too wild...had that been the problem? Had he been too straight? Too strict? Too Catholic? He looked again at the page, was that it? Time? Had he finally broken it? He thought about what that could mean, he thought about Paris...He thought about her!!!

SONG LYRICS

I first saw you selling roses from a rusty old cart
On the streets of Paris somewhere in Montmartre
You stole my watch and I chased you for miles
I said give me your heart I'll give you the world

So, I took you back and we watched the big bang
And we hung out in the gardens of Babylon.
Oh, how you cried as Nero burned Rome
And we did what we could for the wounded at the Somme

Took you back watched the birth of your favourite niece
We discussed philosophy in ancient Greece
But sadly, my friend, time is not yours,
I might live forever but for you there's no cure
But I remember...

So, I took you back and we watched the big bang
And we hung out in the gardens of Babylon.
Oh, how you cried as Nero burned Rome

And we did what we could for the wounded at the Somme

And I miss you and I always will
Because inside me there is a chill
Where my heart it should beat
But instead it is still
Because I loved you
And I always will

So, I took you back and we watched the big bang
And we hung out in the gardens of Babylon.
Oh, how you cried as Nero burned Rome
And we did what we could for the wounded at the Somme

C-29: PANDORA'S MIRROR

Bonsart Bokel

C-29: PANDORA'S MIRROR
BY BONSART BOKEL

UPDATE: C-29 is no longer part of the Association's collection.

Description

C-29 is a large (140 by 50 centimetres) mirror of unknown origin placed within in a dark grey/anthracite oval frame in a Louis Seize-style. The frame is made from mahogany, which is typical for this type of furniture.

In the frame there is a carved text that reads:

"O Fortuna velut luna statu variabilis, semper crescis aut decrescis."

(Oh Fortune, like the moon you are changeable. Ever waxing, ever waning.)

The mirror itself is made from an unknown material and due to its effects, it is extremely difficult to examine, dismantle or take a sample from the mirror's surface. However, an ultralow frequency has been found emanating from C-29, which is thought to be related to its anomalous abilities.

Any non-living, non-human subjected within its line of sight does not provoke any abnormal effects. Special committee Antiquarians put a number of animals in front of the mirror, including a parrot in a cage, Doctor Chartreuse's dachshund and a stray cat. The researchers then observed the animals while not exposing themselves to the mirror's reflection. None of these animals activated C-29's ability, nor did they seem to be in any form of distress. The dachshund tried to play with his reflection, the cat engaged in a staring contest with itself and the parrot only exclaimed profanity and revealed some of Doctor {NAME CENSORED} (alleged) bedroom noises. Various inanimate objects w2ere placed in front of the mirror, like typical household objects, an heirloom once owned by Doctor Chartreuse's mother and one of Doctor Jenever's dollhouses. There were no notable effects.

Side note

It just so happened that in one of the beds inside the dollhouse an instance of c-08 was recharging, which woke up and started to trash the furniture looking for something to drink. This didn't activate C-29 either.

The mirror only becomes active when human subjects make eye contact with their own reflection on the surface of the mirror. People exposed have witnessed a black fog or dark smoke creeping out from underneath the frame towards their reflection. At this point, most witnesses started to feel unwell or terrified as the fog congealed with their reflection blurring the image. Only a few have managed to look away, while most describe a sense of numbness or paralysation causing their eyes to be fixated on the mirror's surface.

After a short moment, the reflection becomes clear again. This final phase of the transformation has been compared to something that emerges from dirty water, after which their own reflections changed into a different version of themselves. For example, their reflections would wear unfamiliar clothes, have a different hairstyle or possess other physical changes; such as scars. The dark fog turns into an environment in which the witness's reflection starts to move about independently and a scenario starts to take place. By this time the witnesses are experiencing a type of 'out of body' experience and are fully emerged into the unfolding events

All the scenarios described by witnesses are wholly unique but always affect them personally. These scenarios show the witnesses' alternate self leading a life that, although very different from their own, are very relatable to them and many witnesses have stated potential possibilities on how these other timelines came about. For example, witnesses have stated seeing deceased relatives or loved ones alive once again, and how these could have affected their lives in a major way. One witness confessed to being a former alcoholic, and he was confronted with a version of himself, "Boozing like it was nobody's business".

Those interviewed all described exposure to C-29 as a negative experience. However, some stated they felt more content with themselves and others desired to 'right some wrongs' or make changes to their lives. About half of the subjects showed signs of depression during the interview and made cynical statements bordering on nihilism. For example, mentions like: no matter what they did or how many lives they would have, they would always fail or end up miserable. Rather these emotional outcomes are intended or side effects can only be speculated upon.

Personal note by Dr Benedictine:

At this point, C-29's origins and purpose remain unknown. It is my personal theory C-29 actually shows alternate versions of those individuals who peer into the mirror. The ultralow frequency emitted by C-29 is potential evidence of that. We know for a fact that alternate versions of individuals exist. If my hypothesis is correct, it might mean we are connected somehow with versions of ourselves in the multiverse. In that case, C-29 might have practical value we are just not aware of… Or maybe it is just some science experiment.

If I am wrong, we may have a mirror that can read our minds and visualises our insecurities and desires.

I don't know which of these two explanations makes more sense. The only way to confirm my hypothesis is by finding one of the people that appeared in the mirror's surface.

Dr Benedictine

History

The existence of C-29 was first recorded in Switzerland when authorities were alarmed by a number of suicides in the wake of a travelling carnival in 1861. Interviews with people from these affected communities revealed there were other individuals who either left town, became depressed or made radical changes to their lifestyle. Some of these individuals were tracked by the Cantonal Police Force who revealed the existence of C-29. The Federal Criminal Police suppressed the news and The Association was contacted.

By the time Associate 178 and 201 arrived at the fair to investigate the suspect sideshow, named Pandora's Mirror, it was already too late. It turned out the cart belonging to the owner of the mirror, Mr Schweizer, had been ransacked by an alleged cult. The federal police used this as an excuse to take Mister Schweizer to a local police station for questioning. According to Schweizer's statement, a group of monkish individuals visited Pandora's Mirror the day prior. These individuals were clearly members of a religious order, but no one could identify their robes. One of them paid for admittance to look into the mirror, which seemed out of character for a friar. This particular individual was also taller than most men and he had his face completely covered by a blue-greyish cloth that didn't even have eye holes. He went inside and came out a moment later seemingly unaffected, which mister Schweizer found remarkable. Then he left without comment, as did the other monks.

The next morning, just before sunrise, Mister Schweizer woke up as he heard somebody force the lock on the door to his cart. Mister Schweizer, according to his own statement, pulled a gun on them. But the large 'faceless monk' of the day before came at him, took his weapon and lifted him up by the throat with one arm nearly suffocating the proprietor. Meanwhile, the monks wrapped the mirror in cloth, loaded it onto a cart and left the scene before anyone could comprehend what was going on. Witnesses claim they saw a suspect wagon heading west, presumably to cross the border to France. This when the federal police handed the case over to the Association.

Associate 178 and 201 continued their investigation, which finally leads them to Saint-Germain-de-Joux. There the gendarmerie confirmed the presence of an unorthodox monastic order in and around the Auvergne-Rhône-Alpes called The Lions of Judah. Associate 178 kept a journal of the investigations in the region.

The following segments are the highlights of the events that occurred between the 4th and 14th of august, 1861. These records were written by Associate 178.

August 4th, 1861

We arrived in Charix today and introduced ourselves as real-estate investors, exploring the French countryside for potential plots of land to build a vacation resort. We brought some surveying equipment for good measure, although neither of us has any idea how to use it. The population of Charix were not that interested in us foreigners and it was somewhat of a challenge to gather information from them. An older man was kind enough to give us directions to the old cloister where the Lions of Judah reside. However, when we asked about its occupiers he acted suspiciously and simply replied with: 'they're just a bunch of monks'. [...]

August 5th

As not to stir up trouble, we remained in town today and attended the Sunday mass. I am not a god-fearing man and was raised a Calvinist. So I tried to get acquainted with catholic customs by book learning. But no literature could have prepared me for the sermon we were about to witness.

Now I am quite certain the Rifts have been brought up by well-intending priests in the past, but when we realised the central topic of the preacher's monologue was actual on the topic of 'Rifts', we became increasingly uncomfortable and neither of us could shake the feeling it was our presence that had roused the subject. But to our surprise, his flock didn't seem all that bothered by the topic and I noticed head nodding in agreement when the priest proclaimed that these portals would lead the faithful to either heaven or hell. If he was just speaking metaphorically, I would probably agree with his claims. The part where he lost me was on breaking the seven seals. Regardless, I was relieved when he announced we would sing the French version of Erstaunliche Gnade.

[...]

It might be my ignorance of the French or Catholic faith, but I don't think this type of religious expression is the norm. Although we both believe that religious worship of the Rifts is inevitable, this appropriation by a catholic congregation feels as if it is part of a larger movement. We wonder if this is the influence of the cult. It would explain all the secrecy.

August 6th

Today we observed the monastery with a modified periscope from a nearby hill to the west of the complex. The structure is typical of 14th-century monasteries of its type, with some modifications made over the centuries. The only space open to the public is a workshop were the friars make spoke wheels, horseshoes, simple tools and farming equipment. In the courtyard, they grow herbs and there is a walled vineyard to the south. Apart from the chapel on the east side of the complex and the sleeping quarter, it is hard to say anything about the internal layout of the complex.

As I observed the complex, my fellow Associate stood on watch, map in hand, pretending to operate the measuring equipment. We tried to get here before the occupants of the convent got up at sunrise. Guess we should have gone during winter.

Regardless of our bad temper, we witnessed something both remarkable and unsettling. As expected, when the first rays struck the cloister, the faithful left their chambers and headed for the chapel to attend the first mass. It included the imposing figure, reaching head and shoulders above all other friars. But his imposing physique could not distract me from another actual glowing individual crossing the courtyard. In the dim morning light, I saw a pale light appear from underneath his robes and cowl, shining so bright it lit the ground before him as he crossed the garden.

But my amazement did not cease as something captured the Glowing One's attention and made him turn around. From behind a tower, another robe-clad 'alien' appeared. The robes struggled to hide its inhuman shape as that moved like a frog that had humps like a dromedary. His body swayed in sync with its covered head hunching forward like that of a crocodile. I can only imagine what its appearance could look like. (Please don't let it be human)

The (assumingly) human cultists bowed their heads politely as they walked by the 'lizard thing' and the Glowing One waited patiently for the Hunchback to approach. While the two were engaged in a lengthy conversation the humped one stuck one its monstrous hands out of its sleeves and revealed its long fingers that sprouted from a withered hand, like branches on a long-dead tree. They talked for three minutes or so before they walked side by side toward the chapel.

We saw the three abnormals a number of times during the day. It seems the Glowing One has a separate plant patch where he grows Saint-Catherine's flowers but there were no remarkable event sightings for the rest of the day.

August 7th

[...] At sunset, we spotted a caravan at the gate of the cloister. A significant number of the cultists were about to leave for what seemed an extended period, based on the provisions being loaded onto the carts. Some members even carried large daggers or blades. At dawn a column of four carts left, leaving a small portion of the community behind.

August 8th

After long deliberation, we decided to explore the interior of the cloister, while the majority of the community is away. While requesting reinforcements to infiltrate the building Associate 201 will follow the caravan and report back through wireless radio.

Not going to lie. I feel out of my depth here. I am an investigative journalist, not a secret agent. This whole affair is starting to feel like a Penny Dreadful. Just like these small wireless devices. Wondering what the world will look like if this technology becomes public.

August 12th

Associate 12, 49 and 154 finally arrived. 12 took command right away. I can't really blame the military man. I explained the situation to him and we agreed it might be best to start the infiltration during the evening mass when the cult-members are occupied. [...]

As the evening mass began, around 8 PM, just after the cult gathered in the main chapel, Associate 49 snuck in. An hour later 49 reported that she explored most the living quarters, stables and supply rooms. The only thing of note was a gymnasium, that the friars used for practising martial arts and an armoury mostly containing obsolete but well-maintained firearms, ammunition and medieval weaponry. But a significant number of weapons were missing from the lockers.

Unfortunately, there was no sign of C-29 or other artefacts, so 49 decided to approach the chapel. 12 allowed this.
[...]

8:34 -A few minutes after 49 reported in, an alarm bell was rung within the cloister. 12 told us to pack our gear onto the horses and wait for 49 to meet us.

8:44 - After 10 minutes, still no sign of 49. 12 was getting restless as two armed friars came to stand in front of the gate. A few minutes later three other cultists left the gate and started searching the area. We assume they are looking for 49, but 12 believed something went horribly wrong. He couldn't finish vocalising his thought until our transponder started to make noise as if somebody was fiddling at the other end of the signal. That's when 12 declared to go in and save 49. I protested that I had no combat experience apart from shooting rabbits. But 12 ignored my complaint and simply told me to watch their back as they went in. Both 12 and 154 mounted their horses and charged in like bloody dragoons. My companions took out two of the three scouts with their revolvers. I froze as last one charged after them like a lunatic. While they took out the guards as they passed the gate the last one kept going after them, screaming like a lunatic. One part of my brain analysed what could happen if I let him be, while the other half struggled with the fact I had to shoot a man to save my comrades. As I aimed my rifle I kept telling myself I shot smaller game at larger distances and finally, mortified, I pulled the trigger.

After that, I hurried to the gate where my fellows left their horses behind. There were more shots and screams as I took shelter near the gate. There I waited for what seemed an eternity. The vegetation in the courtyard was too high to keep an eye on the chapel door but I didn't want to get in the way or stray too far from the horses. The animals were nervous as all hell and I had my hands full preventing them from pulling the reins free from my hands.

Fortunately, my fellows came running back. 49 was walking, be it supported by 154. 12 carried a friar – the Glowing One – over his shoulders. We mounted our horses a ran off. We heard some shots behind us as we left the cloister. It was probably a good thing they used old weapons.

August 13th

[…]

The firefight had attracted a lot of attention and the gendarmerie got involved. They searched the convent in the morning and recovered a number of artefacts, including C-29. The cultists were arrested for theft, smuggling and their illegal weapons. This caused quite a stir within the surrounding communities.

[...]

Currently, Associate 154 is already underway to Lyon to negotiate for the release of the artefacts into Association custody and 12 mentioned both the Glowing One and C-29 will be shipped across the Channel so nobody can come after them. Associate 49 is shaken but not disturbed. The Glowing One is still in our custody, annoyed but compliant. We have not heard back from Associate 201 yet and I am starting to get nervous.   As for why the Lions of Judah wanted C-29. According to 49, the Lions used it in initiation rituals to see if the new members were pious enough, by exposing them to their reflections. I guess it is similar to shamans consuming hallucinogens to go on spirits quests and the like. Well, it has been one hell of a trip.

Aftermath

C-29 was shipped across the Channel. Once delivered the Association conducted only a small number of experiments as time was cut short due to a change in circumstances.

After incident S-78 various items of interest were exchanged with the Lions of Judah, after truce negotiations, which included the release of Associate 201 from their custody. The cult's argument was that the artefact is vital to their initiation ceremonies that prepare novices for 'the battles to come'.

Dr Chartreuse responds to the exchange of C-29

This is outrageous! C-29 is one of the most valuable research assets we have. If our suspicions are correct, we might be able to develop ways to observe other planes without having to traverse any portals. We might even discover how all realities are connected! I insist the Chair reconsiders handing it over to a sect of superstitious zealots who stole the very thing in the first place. Not to mention they are violent. I urge you not to give in to their threats and let us continue our research.

Sincerely,

Dr Chartreuse

Transcript of interview C29-24b.

Interviewer {NAME CENSORED} of Swiss Federal Police. Interviewed Mr Schweizer

[start of segment]

So, Mr Schweizer. Could you tell me again what happened on April 9th?

Oh, please I already told two of your colleagues. How hard can it possibly be to find some monks?

Then tell us again!

You dare? I will not be spoken to that way. I am the victim here!

First, we will talk about your victims Mister Schweizer! Fourteen confirmed suicides. Twenty disappearances. Not to mention the condition of the survivors.

I have had nothing to with any of that! Do you really assume I am murdering my customers?

Listen you! Something changed inside of these people within a very similar timeframe after visiting your sideshow. What did you call it? Pandora's Mirror! Why did you name it that way?

I- This is preposterous. I will not suffer this type of abuse.

Three weeks ago, a single mother of two was dragged lifeless from The Rhone. A day after she visited your show. You want me to tell you about the other thirteen?

Pure conjecture. But fine... My old master named it that way. I simply took over when he died.

Really? How did he die?

He...drowned.

He just, drowned one day?

Yes, he went for a swim and got caught in the current. Got stuck between some driftwood and...

How did he get the mirror?

As I understand it once belonged to a rich industrialist from the United States. The mirror gave him insight into business decisions.

Why did he sell it then?

Well, he died and had no heirs, so his stuff was auctioned off. My master acquired it while on the road in Georgia.

I understand there is a lot of demand for carnivals in the United States. Why come over here?

Well, you can understand the mirror was a hot item.

Did you ever look inside the mirror yourself?

O…Of course.

What wonderful insight did it give you? How to make money at these people expense.

No! Many are grateful for what they have seen. It made them change their lives around. They have told me so themselves!

Or ended their lives it would seem. Fine. What about these monks?

[end of segment]

<u>Interview by Associate 201 with {NAME CENSORED} from Fribourg</u>
[...]

I am aware of the effects of the mirror and what it shows to the people who peer into it. So, could you give me some context first?

My life's story?

If you think that helps.

Fine… I was born in Fribourg. My dad was a drunk who decided he wanted to be a soldier one day and disappeared. My mother thought he died, but no. He took some easy post in some other part of the canton without telling her… I am not sure how my mother made money…Anyway.

In 1847 my home city fell to federal troops. We were promised that the occupiers would leave us alone, but they lied. Dufour's goons started to pillage some of the cities quarters (1). Many fled towards the city hall for safety, but the city council assumed it was an uprising and send in the cavalry to disperse the crowd… My mother got trampled by a horse as she held me to her chest…

I am sorry for your loss.

Well… Sometimes I am happy to see didn't see what I'd become…

Excuse me?

Forget it… You wanted to know about the mirror.

Yes, yes. Please go on. Could you describe the experience?

I went to see the thing during a drunk outing with the lads. Just to be somewhere else other than the house or the mines. I paid for the show expecting some magic trick.

---

[1] General Guillaume Henri Dufour led the federal army of 100,000 soldiers during the Swiss Sonderbund War of 1847. He became one of the founding members of the International Committee of the Red Cross in 1863.

It was so weird. First, it was just me and my reflection, but then the stall's lighting started to become dim and the mirror had this weird darkness about it, like… At first, the mirror seemed to shrink and look more distant. It felt like I started to fall. Then the whole thing went black… My vision became blurred, I lost feeling in my body. I couldn't make sense of what was happening. And then the light came back and then….

[The witness pauses]

I… saw me, but differently. It was like I was floating about in a - place. A nice living room. And I saw myself there.

But it wasn't you, was it?

No. I sure don't dress that fancy. Wasn't me. But it could have been… My father was still there, with my mum…a fucking happy family…their grandchildren, a store with my family's name on it and everything. The kinda life I would have wanted, I guess… Never thought about it… I'm a miner now. My first day, going into the mines was like, welcome to the first day of the rest of your life… Now I just feel like, maybe I could. Would be great to pass on to the children… But how can I do such a thing right? Looking back at the mirror it feels like it's mocking me. Like waking up from a nightmare. But now I feel nothing but doubt and guilt. Like I should be doing better. Should be doing better for my family… I don't know if I hate that mirror more than I hate myself.

What happened after you saw that image?

It showed me something else…but before I go on, you have to understand. After my mother's death, I was put in an orphanage. I would have stayed there but one day my dad decided he wanted me back. I didn't even know who he was. He took me to Bern where he left me in the hands of some trollop he fancied while he was out soldiering. She was just as useless as he was and only saw me as a burden. I think she was relieved when I didn't decide to come home at night... I fell in with a bad crowd. Most of what we did was a petty crime. But Rudy, our boss, had ambitions. He wanted to be part of something bigger. But to be part of that something he needed to build up notoriety.

So, one day our boss decided we should head for a Catholic estate. They were ... just Catholics. We pulled the family and the servants out of bed in the middle of the night and gathered them in the living room. As we ransacked the place Rudy made a game of terrorising them. He, erm, became violent. I just went with the flow when it was agreed to raid the manor. But nicking stuff when nobody is looking is one thing. Looting a place before a family's eyes is another.

The screaming and crying. It all started to get to me that night. At first, I wanted to pull through. Cruelty is the only way to carve out a place in this world Rudy used to say... or something like that. So, I tried to shut out the chaos around me, and searched the cabinets. Then I found this round gold-plated trinket, I thought It was a pocket watch, so I flipped it open. But it turned out to be just a stupid little mirror. However, my reflection made me pause for a moment...

That is when Rudy called my name and I turned around. There he was standing by the man of the house... I don't even know his name. Anyway, Rudy was holding the bat, making threatening gestures towards the already bruised man. "It is time to make these traitors pay," Rudy said as he handed me the club. "Break his legs."

[The witness pauses]

After some hesitation, I grab the weapon and looked at the miserable human, curled up like a frightened animal at my feet. Then I lifted the club above my head and struck. Rudy fell to the ground screaming as he grabbed his shin and I ran off... That very night I left the city and never looked back. I took on farmwork, then left for Fribourg and became a miner. Married my wife and now we have two kids.

Excuse me, you mentioned a second revelation.

I just told you!

Are you implying...?

[The witness slams his fist on the table] You know damn well what I am implying!

I...I see... How did that affect you?

I left that all behind me, I swear! I don't want my children to grow up like I did and get saddled up with so much guilt.

I assure you, I am not with the police... besides you already spoke judgement over your actions. Don't see the point of getting another judge involved.

[End of interview]   [End of this entry]

THE END

ABOUT THE AUTHOR

Late 2012 Bonsart Bokel started a blog called Tupperware Steampunk seeking the answer to a simple question. What makes Steampunk unique? Now he has a YouTube Channel, 'Radio Retrofuture', where he talked to over a hundred guests from all over the world.

His views on Retrofuturism are explained in the Steampunk Beginners Guides videos, hosted by the multi-dimensional curator Dankaert Lexicon. Recently he started a second channel, 'The Retrofuture Research Foundation'.

At the request of RRF Discord-community, Bonsart started writing short stories loosely based on the stories from the SCP forum. These stories became The Association of Ishtar. A clandestine organisation investigating anomalies called Rifts. Portals to parallel versions of Earth. These Rifts are gateways to opportunity, but also harbingers of death. The purpose of the stories is to promote high-concept story writing long writers who are starting out as well as showcasing various ways of worldbuilding.

Both Youtube channels and the Association of Ishtar can be found on www.radioretrofuture.com.

Image of S-78 courtesy of Janneke Stam.
http://jjmstam.nl/

LYRICS: XANDIE RAE

INTRO

Horror can be subtle, or psychologically implied, building up slowly...the power of suggestion giving you the frights...or...

....screw all that, here comes the psycho, wielding a bloodied knife...

SONG LYRICS

When Xandie comes in the dead of night
You best be done with your life
Better hope your affairs are straight
For Xandie don't negotiate

Xandie's blade is called The Nurse
Because its job is drawing blood
Xandie now come take your pain
And see you to another realm

It doesn't matter who you crossed
Your life is now forfeit
When her heels tickle the cobble stones
Pray to go that your alone

Xandie now come bring The Nurse
Come show her where it hurts

She's come to quell your aching heart
And lay your bones upon the hearth
She'll leave a coin on either eye
To fetch you to the other side

She'll leave you pretty for your kin
No blood, no marks upon your skin
Folks will say you died from fright
And they'd be right...

LYRICS: WAGES OF SIN

INTRO

War huh! What is it good for? Well asides elections and business not much...and there's more than one kind of war...there's your standing up to tyrants war, there's the my god's bigger than your god war, there's war for roses and wars that last 100 years, some are fought for right reasons but mostly greed is the motive and sometimes they are even fought for love but rarer still are the wars fought with love...Love is a battlefield , a many splendid thing. It's a drug, it hurts it soars and sometimes it stinks...and occasionally love can tear you apart...

SONG LYRICS

The road to ruin is paved with the backs of the brave
And all the pretty things that they said...
I myself walked that path and indeed
I surpassed all the stupid limits I set...

But if I only knew then what I still don't know now,
Would I plough on ahead, or turn it around...
Would I pick myself up from my deep pile rug
And realise one day, enough is never enough...

The wages of Sin it's a bottle of gin
And memories you'd rather forget...
It's growing old alone, so bitter, so cold...
Add lemon ice and regret...

Older now, but still not the sow,
You predicted upon your retreat…
Oh, and how many times has my vengeful mind,
Had your head on a plate by my feet…

But if I only knew then what I still don't know now,
What could I do? Change?
No diamond or dream, sovereign or bean,
Could buy back even one of those days…

The wages of Sin it's a bottle of gin
And memories you'd rather forget…
It's growing old alone, so bitter, so cold…
Add lemon ice and regret…

So here's to your health my dear
Was it just the dessert you got?
I hear they healthier horses shot…
Yellow Fever, Malaria, diphtheria and gout?
Well, I always said you were a selfish cunt…

But if I only knew then, what I still don't know now,
I'd rather had nothing than live without…
So, here's to us my dear and here's to the past…
And to think they said you and I'd never last…

The wages of Sin it's a bottle of gin
And memories you'd rather forget…
It's growing old alone, so bitter, so cold…
Add lemon ice and regret…

Welcome to SINNEPORT

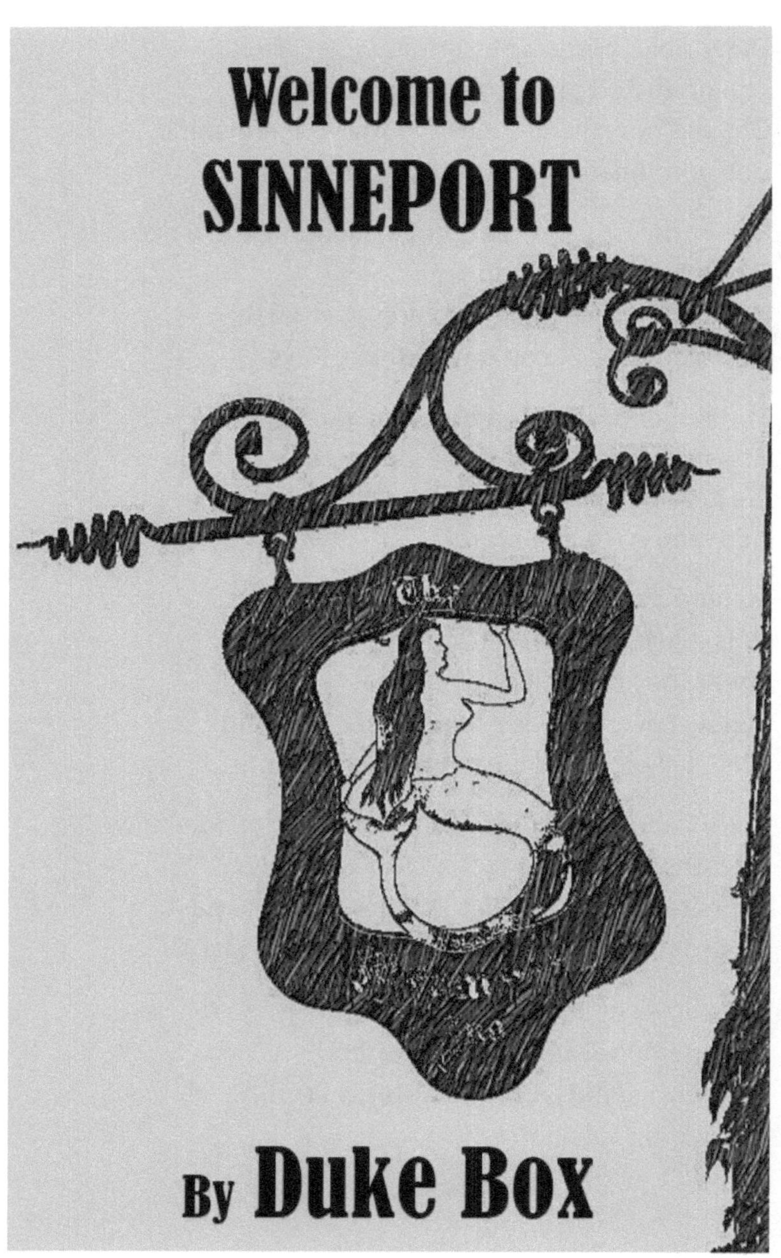

By Duke Box

Duke Box is here, I bring to you,
Greetings and salutations.
So glad that you could join us dear,
For this evening's celebrations.

We find ourselves in Sinneport,
A black heart's smuggling den.

Where we will meet a pirate queen,
Who's fiercer than most men.

A town out of time,
Beyond reason or rhyme,
And lost within a dream.
A time of year, when things appear,
To not be as they seem.

We now seek out, that (in)famous Inn,
For a swift libation.

And there for you a yarn we'll spin,
For your sweet delectation.

And music too, shall guide us through,
A band cast out of time.
I refer of course, to the time-lost crew,
Known as The Dark Design.

But be of good cheer,
And take some beer,
Come enter the Mairemaid Inn.
If you're brave enough,
To turn the page, and let our tale begin.

WAGES OF SIN
Nils Nisse Visser

WAGES OF SIN
A TALE OF THE DARK DESIGN

BY NILS NISSE VISSER

WITH CONTRIBUTIONS BY PENNY BLAKE, NIMUE BROWN & DUKE BOX

ILLUSTRATIONS BY YULIYA NAZARYAN

ROMNEY MARSH
TUESDAY 31 OCTOBER 1871

Scylla Speaks

Damned memories. I reckon the musicians are to blame. I want to drown the lot of them in the vilest mud I can find in the marsh.

Tess Speaks

Though not as commonplace as I would have liked, it wasn't a rarity for a group of wandering musicians to show up at the Mairemaid Inn in Sinneport, offering their skills in exchange for a bite to eat, a drop to drink, a place to sleep, and a handful of coins.

Scylla was wary, but then, she trusted nobody at all. I knew well enough that a good performance could whet appetites and keep the ale flowing.

I wasn't sure about this bedraggled bunch though; they seemed a proper mishmash. The group seemed lost, out of place — perhaps not even fully aware of where they were. And if they were that out of touch, would they know what they'd be doing when they unpacked their instruments?

Three of them stepped forward.

The first had long, wild, silver-streaked black hair. He had a greying moustache and frumious beard. His garments suggested he was a North American frontiersman of sorts, fresh out of the wilderness after a spell of trapping beavers and wrestling grizzly bears.

The second was dressed as an educated gentleman, albeit in khaki tropical gear, pith helmet and all. It was a strange sight to behold on a grey, wet, and chilly English autumn day, more something I would have expected to see worn by a colonial official ambling along the dusty and sleepy main road of a provincial township baking in the midday sun.

The third was clad in old-fashioned sailing gear that wouldn't have looked out of place a century ago – but that wasn't uncommon along the south-east coast. Top hats and bowlers were prevalent along the boulevards of the fancy sea-side resorts, but elsewhere old-fashioned tricorne hats were still stubbornly worn in defiance of high society's fashion fads.
"Are ye any good?" I challenged the musicians. "Or do ye reckon I'm a soft touch?"

The sailor's eyes grew wide with indignation. He indicated the grizzly-man. "Othniel Cope is from Lye Street."

His tone suggested instant awe was a suitable response, but Sinneport was isolated. The town looked much like it did centuries ago, bypassed by most of the wonders brought about by the Age of Steam, and no longer host to a steady flow of travellers who brought us news from the outside world. I shrugged off my ignorance. Since I had never heard of the place, I decided it was safe to assume it wasn't anywhere nearby. "A fair stride from Romney Marsh."

"That may be, Ma'am," the grizzly-man spoke, his accent touched with an echo of Scotland.

"But there are no finer musicians in the realm. We tickle ears, conjure smiles, command laughs, direct feet, blister toes, summon tears, melt hearts, caress souls, and warm loins."

I stared at him. He was possibly not quite right in the head. It all sounded very fine, but I had to make a business decision for which I required facts, not flights of fancies.

"Goody Hawkhurst," the prospector spoke in reasoned tones. "Your reputation as a shrewd…erm…innkeep has spread far beyond the fair town of Sinneport."

"Over the hills and far away," Grizzly-man supplied helpfully. Prospector ignored him and continued, "We are all of us possessed with a healthy sense of self-preservation, Goody Hawkhurst. Thus, we make no idle boasts. We desire to depart these parts with pockets weighed down by fair begotten coin and heads firmly attached to shoulders."

I was pleased with Prospector's response. He demonstrated a good understanding of how things worked out here on this forgotten edge of England and was entirely correct in assuming my wrath was something best avoided. That kind of clarity formed a good basis to build an agreement on.

I thought I heard thunder in the distance, over the bay, and cast an eye at the cloudy sky that held the threat of rain.

"It be coarse weather, ye'd better come in," I told them. "Warm yerself by the fire in the

taproom, and we'll parley terms."

<u>Scylla</u>

Lies! Spies! There's something unsavoury about this lot. Send them on their way, or better yet, give them to me to play with…

<u>Tess</u>

The musicians were allocated a corner of the tap room and began to unpack and tune their instruments. I requested two sets. A short one to earn their supper. A longer one, later this evening, for bed and breakfast.

I wanted to determine if they were anywhere near as good as the wild promises made by Grizzly-man, before committing the inn to a full evening of this odd lot. If they disappointed me, they'd get their supper as promised, and would then be invited to depart with haste.

Other than that, my tap-room was filled with Mairemaid Inn 'regulars'. In these parts it wasn't odd for an inn-keep to employ a dozen or so rough men and women who were never seen to be doing anything other than eating the larder empty and drinking the cellars dry. If they were any good, their other activities remained unseen and unsung.

My lot, the Mudlarks, were good. Best in the business as far as I was concerned. Half of them would have to brave the Rozzers and the chill later that night on a run to the salts of Walland Mush, to collect a crop of tea brought ashore the old-fashioned way, over sea by means of a barque out of Boulogne. The men and women I'd selected for the task would go without hesitation, but I knew they'd be disappointed to miss the music. The early set I asked for also served to let them partake in the entertainment. I looked after my crew, I always had.

There were a few irregulars present as well. If these townsfolk liked what they heard, news of musicians at the Mairemaid would spread through Sinneport like wildfire. Later that night the taproom would fill up with folk seeking to escape small-town life on a dismal autumn's eve.

I sat down by the bar with a gin in hand to observe the band when they launched into their first set.

It was introduced by a man I hadn't noted before, wearing a black coat adorned with pins and badges, an open white shirt, a neatly trimmed extended goatee, begoggled top hat, and round – shaded – spectacles. Seemingly totally oblivious to the fact that the Mairemaid's taproom was relatively empty, he waved his arms enthusiastically and began to speak with enough volume to be heard at the sold-out matinee in the massive tent of a travelling circus.

"Ladies and Gents. Boys and Girls. Scaddles and Scoundrels – do heed my words as I, the one and only Duke Box and incomparable vox of—"

He was interrupted by a grizzled fisherman who shouted: "Pize, they got one of them at the Sea Pook Tavern yonder in Winchelsea."

Duke Box parried fluently: "O ho good sir! But you are mistaken. I know of the dreary den of despair to which you refer, and they don't have a Duke Box with a 'D' as is only proper, but a jukebox with a 'J'. It's a gaudy musical trinket that someone stuck gears, bells, lamps, and whistles on. No sir, I am the Duke of Box Hill, I am the original steampunk gent, I am the jester who dances on the road of bones. And so, I beg you good people, charge your cups, be it with ale, mead, or Brandywine. Come on now folks, do drink up, as playing for you, come here from hither and thither and then, we have none other than: The Dark Design!"

The musicians launched into their first song and I was pleased to note that they knew their instruments and handled them efficiently. The band certainly judged their audience well, choosing a popular favourite to kick things off. 'Bell Bottom Trousers' was received with cheers and had all singing along.

Singing bell bottom trousers,
Coat of Navy-blue
Let him climb the rigging
Like his daddy used to do!
Then early in the morning
The sailor he arose
Saying here's a two-pound note
My dear, for the damage I've done
If you have a daughter
Bounce her on your knee
If you have a son...
SEND THE BASTARD OUT TO SEA!

The Mairemaid Inn shook as if it had flown headlong into turbulent air when just about everyone in the taproom roared out the last line.

<u>Scylla</u>

Fee-fol-diddle-fee-dum, heigh-ho-a-nonny-no. Remember that French cloud buccaneer the Portuguese boiled alive on Playatown Plaza? To serve as an example to the rest of us? He sang prettier than this lot when that water started heating up.

Do you reckon mud boils? That's an interesting thought, surely it will. We could experiment. We should experiment. In the meantime, there is a particularly putrid mud pool near Jury's Gap, large enough to fit the whole band. Weigh them down with shot…

<u>**Tess**</u>

Continuing to display insight of the crowd they were playing to, enthusiasm waxing as if the band fed on the energy of their audience, the musicians launched into a rendition of 'Smuggler'.

The fiddle-dee-diddle part Scylla complained of was still an aspect of the music, but some of the musicians at the back of the group had produced different instruments, some quaint and odd looking. The use of strange instruments added fresh life to the old song, and they did something else I couldn't quite put a finger on, something that changed the rhythm and lent the familiar tune a catchy unpredictability.

I'd always liked this song and began to tap my feet on the floor.

Oh my love, you have a cosy bed,
Cattle you have ten,
You can live a lawful life,
And live with lawful men.
I must make do with nothing,
While there's foreign gear so fine,
Must I drink but water,
When France is so full of wine?

<u>**Scylla**</u>

More fol-die-diddle-dol-diddy. Unlike Tess, I'm paying attention. There is something strange about that band. It's something more than just the dress sense of the three odd frontmen, not to mention that peculiar impression they give of being here – but not quite here.

I try to count them and in doing so discover a source of strangeness. The musicians are impossible to count. The first time I count nine. Double-checking, I count ten. Then there are nine again, followed by eleven. Somehow, they are drifting in and out of the collective, and no matter how sharply I watch them, I can't see anyone arriving or departing from the group. Yet their numbers change.

I can't explain it. Then again, I don't need to. It's clearly unhealthy. They're warlocks of some sorts, sorcerers. Don't tell me these don't exist, I've seen things…far south of here, that much is true. But this has the same feel. These kinds of folk don't go anywhere without a reason and the world has taught us not to expect any kindness from strangers.

To Jury's Gap with them, I say. Weigh them with shot. Enough weight to drag them down into the mud, but not enough to hasten their ordeal. How they will squirm! Until the unrelenting inevitability of their impending death extinguishes the last remnant of desperate hope in their eyes. Always a touching moment. They'd be singing a different tune then, I'm sure.

Free Traders drink of the Frenchman's wine,
And the darkest night is Owling time.
Air Fleet Rozzers prowling astern,
Landsharks awaiting beyond our bow.

Tess

I couldn't resist, no-one in the taproom could, joining in with the last two lines of the chorus.

It's a Free Trader's life for me,

Riding the clouds, like an outlaw free.

The lines revealed a division within the ranks of my Mudlarks. Most, the locals, emphasised the first line.

Four – five if I included myself –, put heart and soul into the second line. We sang "riding the clouds like an outlaw free" with that fierce power nostalgia can have, then glanced each other's way, exchanging knowing, barely discernible smiles.

These four I had known the longest. They had crewed for me in the south, on my airship, a converted sky-schooner called *The Parseval.* None of them required work when we had returned to Blighty, the hold filled with the accumulated treasure of twelve year's plunder. They could have retired but had chosen to stay with me and join my new profession. They were in the business for the sheer joy of it, and loyal to a fault.

Not among this tight core, in the ranks of the native Free Traders instead, was my daughter Nellie. All of nineteen years old and filled with that boundless optimism young folk have when they believe the world to be at their feet, the future promising opportunity, rather than pain, heartache, and worry.

When at last the sun comes up,
Run's crop safely stored,
Like sinless saints to church we go,
God's mercy to afford.

I looked at Nellie's cheerful face, framed by long red hair like mine.

I felt pride because of who she'd become. Intelligent, independent, compassionate, strong, and blessed with a healthy sense of humour.

I also beheld her with some sadness, because it was indeed the Free Trader's life for Nellie as she had just joyously sung out.
It had been my desire that she learn a useful trade. I had often told her that most unhappy women I knew were dependent on men and caught in that dependency squirming and wriggling like a eels in a trap. The lesson was to have a trade and income, it allowed me, and later upon my passing Nellie, to dictate

terms. Nellie had taken to inn-keeping and Free Trading like a gull to the sky, but sometimes I felt that I restricted her options. The arrangement kept Nellie from a life of continuous risk which I wanted her spared from, but which I myself missed with every fibre of my being.

It's the finest French for communion wine,
The parson drinks it too,
With a sly wink prays, 'Lord.'

Another thundering, inn-shaking finish.

FORGIVE THESE MEN AND WOMEN,
FOR THEY KNOW NOT WHAT THEY DO!

<u>**Scylla**</u>

Listen to them roar. In celebration of their own exploits which they no doubt consider derring-do heroism. Bah, humbug. Furtive scurrying about in the dark like hungry bilge rats in an empty hold. Running away from danger all the while, instead of facing it head on and letting gun and blade decide the outcome.

Now the sorcerers have launched into a song about writers, raising a glass to toast them even.

I toasted a writer once. It hadn't been my intention, we tended to leave passengers of seized airships unharmed. Unless they put up resistance. This bespectacled fellow, was holding on to his leather briefcase with both arms, shouting that I couldn't have it. It's hardly a clever thing to say to a pirate, is it? I made a grab for it. The idiot slashed out wildly with a knife, so I ran him through with my sword. Even as he was dying, on the ground and choking on his blood, the writer was staring desperately at his briefcase when I opened it, raising a trembling hand as if to reclaim it.

I never understood why. There was nothing of any value in there, just thousands of sheets of paper, all covered with meticulous scribbles. We consigned them to the heads on board *The Parseval*. I swear we wiped our arses with that stuff for nigh on a month, there was so much of it.

Remember *The Parseval*? You were afraid of nothing. Intercept, grapple, board, and damn the consequences. The infamous 'El Escorpion', feared along the length of the South Atlantic and Pacific coasts of Latin America, Scourge of the Caribbean. Why, the mere sight of *The Parseval* swooping down from the clouds and hoisting her colours – the white winged skull on a black field – was enough to subdue most prey into instant submission, lowering their flags, cutting their engines, and waiting passively to be boarded and parted from cargo and treasure.

Why? What on earth drove you to give up the carefree life? Riding the clouds like an outlaw free?

Tess

I continued looking at Nellie, a prime reason for retiring from my earlier career. Scylla mostly remembered the glamorous parts of it. The sheer triumph of outsmarting, outflying, and outfighting a foe. The joy of landing on a deserted stretch of tropical beach, *The Parseval's* hold filled choc-a-bloc with the contents of the larders and bars of a luxury long-haul aeroliner – good for a fortnight's or more wild feasting on warm nights beneath the bright stars of the southern hemisphere.

Scylla didn't remember the hungry, lean days. The nightmares after a crew did resist, forcing us to hack and hew our way through them to get at the loot. Proud men and women pissing

98

and shitting themselves in terror, screaming or whimpering for their mothers at the end. The ever-present danger of betrayal when you're living with a price on your head, aware that it's all borrowed time.

I know my history. Our names echo down the centuries. Glossed over to make the anomaly of our existence something to be marvelled at. Transformed to change our harrowing motivations into a noble calling of sorts. Cleansed of our foulest deeds, or not, depending on whomsoever tells the tale.

Those who call us Queens of the Sea, or Queens of the Sky, often neglect to add that our average reigns were short, the years counted on one hand, sometimes two. Most often it's an inglorious end. There's nothing majestic about dancing the gallows jig, with a hemp necklace around your neck and the contents of bladder and bowels running down your kicking legs. Nor is there much grace dying in the corner of a shanty reeking with the stench of gangrene, screaming at the pain to go away, begging a crewmate to employ gun or blade to provide a merciful end.

I'd already beaten the odds when I gave birth to Nellie and had accumulated a tidy fortune in the process. Earlier on in my career I would have scoffed at the notion of quitting while ahead, but the arrival of a child had changed my priorities. Before, I had cared not whether I lived or died, which lent me reckless courage that is becoming in a Queen of the Sky. Afterwards, I wanted to live. Not so much for my sake as for my child's.

Fate had decreed that I myself started life in an orphanage, the lowest of the low, almost certainly destined for the short and violent life of a street girl. I'd escaped that prospect when I was thirteen, by stowing away on a cargo-zep, unaware of the destination of the airship and caring not, as long as it took me out of England.

I'd ended up in Portuguese America, the colony of Parolando, where I'd found gainful employment in the galley of a Dutch privateer on an air-flute called *De Zuidvloed*. It had been a modest start, but I'd made the best of it, and had never looked back until Nellie was born.

I didn't want her to grow up an orphan. Nellie's father had died before she was born. He had been a handsome, if somewhat dim fellow with a West Country drawl, who had got himself captured by Spanish bounty-hunters. They had tortured him. To his credit, he had died beneath their knives without uttering so much as a whisper regarding my whereabouts. To the bounty-hunters he had been a means to come one step closer to earning the significant bounty on my head. To me, he had been a pleasant companion, who had surprised me by his willingness to die to protect his unborn daughter; a sacrifice I reckoned I should honour by ensuring the baby had at least one living parent left to guide her to adulthood in a hostile world.

We'd flown *The Parseval* back to Blighty, where I had paid off my crew. Every share had been enough for a comfortable retirement. As skipper, my share had been larger still. I could have lived out the rest of my life in idleness, but that kind of life would have sent me crawling up the walls screaming. Instead, with Nellie in my arms and in the company of the four crew who had refused to part ways from me, I had gone back home, to Sinneport at the eastern tip of Sussex. None remembered me, and why should they? I had been a scrawny urchin when I had fled. I returned a mature woman, with a daughter and a fortune. I bought the Mairemaid Inn and busied myself running the inn and directing the Free Trading activities of my Mudlarks. There was some risk involved, but astonishingly low compared to the uncertainty of life as an airship pirate.

Scylla

Damn, but the bastards are seductive in their play. I cannot help but tap my feet on the floor and rap my fingers on the bar top as they launch into a reel that happens to be Nellie's favourite.

Oh come list a while, and you shall hear,
By the rolling sea lived a maiden fair.
Her mother learn'd her the Free Trade,
Skirring the night sky, of none afraid.

Tables and benches are moved to the side of the room, regulars and irregulars mix on the improvised dance floor. It's more dee-diddle-pee-piddle to be sure, not how we danced down south, but it's impossible not to be impressed by the frenetic energy that fills the taproom.

Now, in Owler's clothing the maid did go,
Dress'd as Free Trader from top to toe,
Her beloved mother was the only care,
Of this skirring maiden who ne'er despair'd.

My eyes are fixed on Nellie. No song could be more apt for her and the young woman seems to know it. There's fierce joy on her face as she twirls and swirls across the improvised dance floor, eyes fixed on the broad-shouldered and handsome young man she's dancing with; Sam, one of the sons of the Old Bell's innkeep.

When did Nellie start to take an interest in these things? I often accuse Tess of being too sentimental, but now find myself surprised that the little girl I've seen grow up here at the Mairemaid has outgrown my perceptions. Watching Nellie dance with Sam leaves me in little doubt that Nellie has grown up. The way those two are looking at each other, are thrilled by the other's brief touch in dance, and the energy that radiates between them as tangible as sparks exploding from a smith's hammer striking the anvil – all of it leaves me in little doubt as to what those two will likely be up to after Nellie returns from the salts with the crop of tea.

I grin.

Good girl.

With her pistols load'd she went aboard.
By her side hung a glittering sword.
In her belt two daggers; well-armed for war
Was this fierce maiden who never fear'd a scar.

Tess

I was pleased to see Nellie happy but it was a poignant moment too. Truly Nellie was ready to start a life of her own. We had much in common, and over the last few years had become accomplices and business partners, as well as mother and daughter. None of that would fade, yet I felt like I was losing something precious.

There was a brief sense of failure too, as a mother. Possibly this was one of those times when some wise motherly advice was to be imparted, but what could I possibly say to Nellie?

Now they had not skirred far from the land,
When a strange sail brought them to a stand.
"Those are Coastguard sky-sharks," the maid did cry,
"Let the bastards have it, kill them or in trying die!"

Scylla

Easy. Tell her men have their uses, but it's best not to get too attached to them. They are foolish creatures. Given a hint of possible glory, they'll rush off to war and get themselves killed. Perceiving a slight to their honour, they will insist on drunkenly staggering out of whatever tavern they're in to have their face beaten to pulp outside. Granted the merest glimpse of breast or buttock, and they'll forget yours quicker than it takes for their unfastened breeches to fall to the ground.

They kill'd those sky-sharks and took their store,
And soon return'd to old Enga-land's shore.
With a keg of brandy she walk'd along,
Did this fearless maiden, and sweetly sang a song.

Tess

Could I argue with Scylla's cynicism? Were the lessons I'd learned apt for my daughter? I sighed. If Nellie wanted a bit of fun with Sam, that was her right and it was what young folk do. But what if she was to lose her heart to him? Who was I to argue? There were some who grew happily old together, though outnumbered I reckoned by those who grew old together with weary resignation. Then there were all too many whose hearts were crushed, splintered, rendered, or otherwise smashed into smithereens. Was there a worse pain to bear? Was it not better to lose a hand to sabre's slash, or a leg to a cannonball?

My eyes caught those of Pug, one of my loyal Parsevals. Grinning, as if he knew what I was thinking, he raised the stump of his left arm, which now ended in a glinting, steel hook. That had been that French frégate-de-l'air which reckoned with military arrogance that *The Parseval* was easy prey. They had been caught by surprise when I turned about and drove our outgunned sky-schooner straight at them at full speed to board them. The French had put up a stiff resistance, leaving Pug with his 'scratch', as he called his artificial appendage.

I grinned back at Pug. At least a broken heart could be pieced together again, in a fashion. And then fortified to protect it from further harm. That had been my way. I'd formed temporary alliances, all our energy spent in a few magical weeks, feasting around a fire on a starlit beach, sneaking off to frolick in the surf, and then give in to feverish passion on the warm sand. It would always be over by the time *The Parseval* ascended the sky once more, letting me focus on the task at hand without distraction. Free.

Nellie's father had lasted longer than most, simply because I was with his child. There had been one exception, the reason I'd encased my heart with a barrier of steel and rigidly regulated my passions in the first place.

I pushed the thought of him, the image of his face, away. Some memories are best forgotten.

The musicians finished 'Smuggler's Daughter' and had come to the end of their first set. The audience cheered and hooted appreciation. Grizzly-man approached me, a satisfied grin on his face.

"Well, Goody Hawkhurst?" He inquired.

"Ye've earned a hearty meal," I replied. "And twould please me to hear more tonight. One of my folk will show ye yer sleeping quarters, and arrange food."

He shrugged as if that wasn't of importance. "I meant the music, Goody Hawkhurst. What did you think of our music?"

I shrugged in return. "Like I said, ye've earned a bettermost meal and a comfortable bed."

Out of the corner of my eye I caught Nellie saying her goodbye to her young man, before departing the taproom with half-a-dozen Mudlarks in tow. They'd be heading down to the cellars to prepare.

Grizzly-man looked disappointed. "You speak of our art like a commodity."

"Ye've offered it to me as such," I countered, but then relented. "But if it pleases ye, ye're good enough to play at an inn where the Bard himself stayed and performed."

"I'm aware of it and honoured," Grizzly-man replied, before confusing me with utter nonsense. "I recall that performance, it wasn't half bad, considering Will had a bit of a cold and a drop more to drink than he ought to have. But our set just now...?"

"My heart only beat faster as a natural response to any well-timed riff," I told him. "There were naun shedding of tears, nor melting of hearts."

He bowed his head a little, seeming to perceive I'd already been as generous as I was going to be in my praise. "The lack of hot tears and cracked hearts, Ma'am, was out of consideration of your exalted self, a matter of courtesy, I assure you."

I laughed. "Courtesy be damned, troubadour. Do yer best I say. I tell ye what, if ye manage to move me as such in yer second set, I'll pay ye double the coin agreed upon."

"As you wish." The sparkle in his eyes told me that he had accepted the challenge. I could have warned him that scaling the cliffs at Beachy Head on a stormy night would have been an easier task than laying siege to my soul, but reasoned it was far better to have him and his musicians give it their all later.

Scylla

I make my way to the cellars, the oldest part of the inn. It's a labyrinth of passageways and ancient-barrel-vaulted chambers, including a central chamber we use to plan and debrief sea, sky, and land runs. Nellie and the half-dozen Mudlarks have just finished preparing for their run out into Walland Mush.

It's customary for Free Traders to wear a disguise of sorts when out and about. Usually this disguise isn't much more than a large scarf that can be wrapped around the face, or even just a small jute sack with holes cut out for eyes and mouth. In a similar vein Free Traders use a code name, rather than their own during an operation.

The Mudlarks take it a step further, following the example set a century before by that parson from Dymchurch. The churchman had turned into a Free Trader chief at night, riding around Romney Marsh with his men in elaborate disguises that lent supernatural terror to their appearance.

I reckon the parson had understood a thing or two about the human mind and knew a disguise serves more purpose than just hiding an identity – it can also allow the wearer to assume a different character, one who is perhaps braver and more audacious than they'd normally be. Added to that was the natural tendency of folk to be frit of the dark and be prone to all sorts of superstitions. The marsh folk spoke of the Dymchurch gang as hellish demons. It's not a bad reputation to have when your aim is to go about your business undisturbed.

Nellie – Neeva now to use her Free Trader code name – and the others have donned long dark cloaks. They've daubed their faces with white paint, with black circles around their eyes and black lines to denote nostril slits and teeth, to create a skull-like impression. Most are also wearing headgear that makes it look like as if they have tusks, horns, or antlers.

Even though I know fully well these are but disguises, and in fact it was I who had devised them, I still feel a chill steal through my bones when I enter the chamber and see all the animated, grinning skulls in the flickering candlelight.

I talk them through the mission. It's as routine as they come, and old-fashioned because the goods are being delivered by sea, rather than through the air as has become custom. Had that been the case, I would have donned my Mairemaid of

Sinneport disguise and flown out with the Mudlarks on board one of our cloud-ketches, if only just to feel a feeble echo of past adventures on *The Parseval.*

As it is, the mission is ideal for Nel…Neeva to lead, though I remind them of the dangers of complacency. Sinneport's police constables will be at the Mairemaid tonight, in a drunken stupor, Tess will see to that. But there are other Rozzers to be mindful of out in the marsh. Not particularly brave ones, but they do carry loaded guns and are ill-trained in the use of them. It wouldn't be the first time a fire fight ensued simply because a Rozzer panicked at the sight of a disguised Mudlark emerging from mist or darkness.

Wishing Neeva and the Mudlarks good luck, I bid them be on their way, and they make their way into one of the secret tunnels.

<u>**Tess**</u>

I sent instructions to the kitchens that there'd be extra mouths to feed, about a dozen of them, though I wasn't entirely sure exactly how many musicians travelled in the band.

I ordered extra casks of cider and ale to be brought up from the cellars, anticipating a busier than usual evening. The remaining Mudlarks went down there as well, to mix taxed gin and Brandywine in equal measures with a recent night-time crop of Dutch Gineva and Madeira wine. The taste would be much improved as I only purchased the best for illicit import. The price would plummet because the good stuff, free of excise duties, was by far cheaper to obtain. The Mairemaid's reputation of good booze for low cost kept the inn running at a healthy profit.

I sent an errand boy to invite the town's police constables, armed with the promise of free drinks for our gallant law-enforcers. I also had a few kegs of the 'special stuff' brought up, the only partially diluted and therefore highly potent spirits I liked to serve gentlemen in uniform, in honour of their bravery in keeping Romney Marsh safe from undesirables.

All of that done, I joined the remaining Mudlarks for our evening meal and tried to relax, though that was never easy when Nellie was out on a run.

I reminded myself that she was capable and competent. Moreover, my Parsevals Pug and McFeck were by her side and Nellie was clever enough to rely on their experience and advice. Both men had known Nellie for all her nineteen years, were filled with paternal adoration of my daughter, and would die protecting her if that was needed.

<u>**Scylla**</u>

The band of travelling sorcerers, rather than finding themselves choking and gagging on vile mud as is still my advice, are given a generous meal and ample time to rest from their travels and first set.

They look refreshed, as, one by one, they start to reappear in the tap room, which is gradually filling with irregulars from town, in a mood of happy anticipation.

We are called away, alerted by those posted on the bell tower of St Mary's. Something is wrong out in the marsh. The church isn't far away, and we are used to climbing the narrow, almost tunnel-like lower stone stairs of the tower, and then the lofty and apparently ever more rickety wood ones that take us all the way to the rafters of the steeple. The view afforded by the parapet walkway is breath-taking by day, and even in the night's darkness there is a sense of great space all around.

The lookouts point, needlessly so. Gazing south-east, out over Walland Mush, there'd normally be a few clusters of lights denoting marsh villages, hamlets, and farms. It's different tonight. I retrieve my spy glass and train it on the salts between Jury's Gap and the village of Lydd. From what I can make out, four airships are flying low over the salts, each one equipped with multiple search lights, the beams of which are sweeping to and fro. From a distance, it looks as elegant as a stylised dance of sorts, but for anyone down on the ground, hunted by those beams, it must be terrifying. Worse, every now and then I can see prolonged bursts of fire from the bows of the airships. I can't hear them, but my memory provides the deathly rattle of Gatling guns.

Nellie and her Mudlarks are out there. The crop of tea was due to be collected right where those airships are prowling the salts. It's strange, for neither the Coastguard nor the Royal Aero Force normally operate in this manner, we aren't prepared for this.

I clench my jaws. Whatever is happening out there, will be over by the time we'd get there were we to rush out of Sinneport now. We can only wait, and hope that Nellie, Pug, McFeck, and the rest are keeping their heads low.

Even as I watch, the airships disengage and depart. Are they giving up their search? Or have they found and eliminated what they were looking for?

Tess will be taking this hard, no doubt. I'm made of sterner stuff. No matter how safe we want Nellie to be, Free Trading does entail risks, and our lass was bound to face a baptism of fire sooner or later.

We return to the Mairemaid, in time for the closing chorus of the shanty 'Blow the Man Down', the entire taproom singing along with gusto.

Oh, blow the man down, bullies, blow the man down
To me way aye blow the man down
Oh, blow the man down, bullies, blow him away,
Give me some time to blow the man down!

Tess

A woman stepped forward from the obscure group behind the band's three frontmen. I hadn't spotted her before, which was odd because of her distinct appearance. She wore a long, hooded cape, coloured a rich dark green with curling ivy stems and leaves embroidered on it in lighter shades of green. Pushing the hood back, the woman revealed a Wodewose half-mask, akin to the Green Man face, but consisting entirely of different types of leaves in their autumnal red, orange, brown, and yellow colours.

She commanded instant respect; you could have heard a sliver of Spanish silver fall on the taproom's pavestones. Folk around here go to church, but they haven't forgotten their far older roots. Most communities around here still know how to find their way to the Wise Folk, and when one of the Wise Folk desires to speak, folk listen.

She began to speak in a soft voice. "While there are green leaves on the trees, something of summer remains. When the last leaves have gone, winter has come. All Hallow's Eve falls on the tipping point between the two. The threshold between seasons, the threshold between life and death. Tonight, we remember our dead."

She began to sing, accompanied only by the beat of a hand-held drum.

Set a place at the table
With food and drink aplenty
An extra cup, an extra plate
For the dead but not forgotten.

I fought back a rising panic caused by the persistent notion that Nellie was in trouble out in the mush, and might even now be in that other world, even as the veils between the land of the living and the otherworld were lifting.

Not all that many hours ago, I had been content as content could be. Proud of my independence, proud of my achievements. No longer the mistress of two oceans, that much was true, but not unhappy to weave a web of trade, both legal and illicit, across Romney Marsh.

None of that mattered if I lost Nellie. I'd be left with nothing at all. My daughter who I had so admired on the improvised dance floor not long ago, the passion of her dance with Sam another trigger: Memories of long, hot nights a lifetime ago.

The night has come for waking
As the dead they move among us
Come through the veil of passing years.

The dead, or our memories of them? Memories were a strange thing. I was at times surprised by the sheer power memories could bring about – transforming my experience of reality even; reducing the here and now to an insubstantial, dreamlike state and lending the there and then a vivid and imperative validity.

Sometimes, on an errand in town, braving cold wind and persistent rain, the merest hint of a particular smell would transport me thousands of miles and a lifetime away. Once more I'd feel baked by a tropical sun at the hustle and bustle of a market resplendent with hundreds of sights, sounds, smells…so real I would momentarily forget the misery of English weather, the responsibilities that weighed me down, the worries that kept me awake at night. Once more carefree and unconcerned about consequence, living from day to day, port to port, prey to prey.

Sounds too, could be a powerful trigger of memories. A door slammed too loud in my vicinity, and I'd be instantly alert, alive to the tiniest detail of my surroundings, feeling naked and vulnerable without the familiar weight of sword and pistols ready to snatch from my baldric. Add to that the ambiance that could be evoked by music and…

Scylla

…Some memories are best forgotten, tucked away in a dark nook of the mind behind lock and key. When they do emerge, they can do so with the unstoppable power of the fiery and sulphurous eruption of a Chilean volcano, not merely content to be present in awareness, but eager to claim their victim whole…

Tess

…and it was hardly a matter of dark design that my mind desired to dwell in times past, upon those now gone from us…

I see the smoke that circled him
I hear his footsteps, I speak his name
Hail to you upon this night
For a time you are returned.

Was it a good sign that it wasn't Nellie who appeared through the misty shrouds of memory and lives past? Instead, it was him. I spoke his name…

Scylla

…You speak his name. I speak his name. We speak his name, our voice one and the same…

Tess

"Hawkeye."

I will return to you so long as seasons keep on turning.
All Hallow's Eve will call me...
...and I will rise again.

Scylla

They had held back in their first set, those damned sorcerers, now revealing – and unleashing – a powerful conviction in song and music, using those strange instruments and non-native rhythms to cast a spell upon their hapless audience. The Samhain song was followed by a Sussex lament, a favourite, yet the way of delivery made it sound like a whole new song, the impact an emotional experience anew. Their spell cast, Tess succumbed to it all too quick. I tried to wrestle control from her, but that she wouldn't allow.

As I was a-walking down by the seashore
Where the wind and the waves and the waters roar
There I heard a sad voice make a pitiful sound
Of the wind and the waves and the waters all 'round

Tess

His real name was John Kittyhawk, but he had been known as Cap'n Hawkeye.

How young we'd been, he and I. How naively convinced our love would last forever.

We had met along the shores of Rio de La Playa. I'd moved up since mustering on the Dutch air-flute, already in command of *The Parseval*, carving a bloody name for myself and my crew.

Hawkeye was a privateer, in command of the sloop *Firebrass*, not quite in the service of the King and supremely confident on his quarterdeck. I taught him to skirr the skies and was astonished by his natural aptitude for flying. Hawkeye was one of a rare breed: A Wind Reader, able to perceive movements in the sky which most cannot.

He taught me how to dance. Not the European dances in the clubs of Playatown or Decosta, where I could not venture, nor would have wanted to. Instead he took me to secret inland locations, where natives and slaves met for social occasions of their own – borrowing European traditions to add to the fusion of their own native styles. A whole new music, a whole new type of dancing.

No rigid protocols, no fixed sequences. Instead, we stepped to the music and the rest was improvisation in open or closed embrace, dancing chest-to-chest, thigh-to-thigh, hip-to-hip. It was called the tangomão or tambo, frowned upon by most Europeans, but Hawkeye and I lived for those nights of non-stop dancing and we were made welcome.

We taught each other other things too, in the privacy of our cabins aboard *Parseval* or *Firebrass*, or on lonely stretches of beach, lost and delirious in each other's arms, wanting more of the other, needing more of the other. Everything felt right, everything felt in place, everything felt whole.

During the brief spells that our immediate desires were sated, we schemed and plotted. With our combined skills and both aerial and naval means at our disposal, we were nigh unstoppable.

We jokingly called these our Hawkish ventures, playing on our names: Kittyhawk, Hawkeye, and Hawkhurst.

Drunk on love, our souls as one and feeling invincible, we would have laughed, Hawkeye and I, had anyone told us it would all end in bitter tears.

Then she stretched forth her arms and made a great leap
From the rocks that were high to the water so deep
Saying the shells of the oysters shall make me a bed
And the shrimps in the ocean wriggle over my head.

Hawkeye and I had been planning the ultimate caper, one that would see us so rich we'd never have to work again. A Spanish ship loaded with gold. We spent hours poring over sea-charts, stolen timetables, and other titbits of information we'd gotten

120

our hands on. Sitting naked on his bunk or mine, skins still moist and glowing after lovemaking, sipping dark rum, plotting, and scheming – dreaming of a quiet life together, even though both of us were far too restless for a quiet life. Not back then, at any rate, and I still struggle to make it work in a way that leaves my mind untouched.

We were caught by surprise when the announcement came that London and Madrid had cobbled together a peace treaty, ending all hostilities forthwith. I couldn't have cared less, but Hawkeye did.

"I'm a privateer, not a pirate," he told me. "I'll fight the King's enemies, none other."

Being a pirate, that did not sit well with me. Nor his assumption that I would follow his lead, giving up the life I'd carved out for myself at great risk. My freedom.

We disagreed. We argued. We pleaded. We shouted. We cursed. We wept. We went our separate ways.

The Spanish ship sailed across the Atlantic without incident.
Our plan had required a cunning sea captain and *The Firebrass*.
Impetuous as I was, I wasn't willing to risk *The Parseval* and
crew in a hare-brained and hasty improvisation. Nor was I
willing to forgive Hawkeye for abandoning our original plan.
Abandoning what we had together.

Now every night at eight bells they appear
When the moon is shining and the waters are clear
Two constant lovers with all their young charms
Rollin' over and over - locked in love's arms.

Scylla

It was a brilliant and fool proof plan.
More than that, it was our brainchild;
it was a symbol of our union, which
he rejected out of sheer stupidity.
He was an idiot. You, we, I…should
have never trusted him again. But
you did, didn't you? You insisted,
even though I told you not to.

Crying: Oh my love's gone, the youth I adore
He's gone and I never shall see him no more.

Tess

I wanted the memories to stop – I knew where they were
headed and dreaded having to relive the pain.

Stop they did, just as my heartbeat did, albeit briefly, when one
of the Mudlarks I'd posted outside to keep watch came into
the taproom and made straight for me.

The band launched into a song about a Red Queen. The Mudlark had the sense to walk calmly. Rushing might draw undue attention to herself. Not that the local constabulary, all present, would notice, as they were practically comatose after generous rounds of the special stuff, but it always pays to be careful, if only to remain in the habit of doing so.

I kept my face neutral, to hide enormous relief upon hearing Nellie was alive and well.

"Pug follows with ponies and crop," the woman said in a low voice. "Neeva and McFeck rode ahead with the children, they be taking them to the Blue Room."

"Children? What children?"

The woman shrugged. "A boy and a girl. Chopback and Fishgut. That be all I ken."

Like the Mudlarks were from Sinneport, the Chopbacks hailed from Hastings and the Fishguts from Rottingdean.

Rottingdean!

Hawkeye was from Rottingdean. It might mean nothing, but on this night of all nights? After just having been exposed to the raw memory of him?

I left the taproom and made my way upstairs to the Blue Room. McFeck stood by the closed door. There was a pile of torn and stained garments by his feet.

"Was it bad out there?" I asked, looking at the garments.

"Nae fur us," McFeck answered. "But the bairns hae been tae hell an back. Brave, wee, scrawny things they are."

He opened the door and I stepped through.

There were two single beds in the room, tucked into corners and opposing each other. Each bed was occupied by a child, both unclothed. One of the inn's maids sat beside the boy, tending a cut across his chest. Nellie sat by the girl, who lay on her tummy, face towards the wall in the far corner. Nellie was cleaning a nasty scrape across her shoulder.

I judged the children to be ten or eleven years old. They were both covered with bruises and cuts, and both unresponsive to the treatment of their injuries.

"They're fast asleep," Nellie told me. "Goody Tumtops said they were all jawled out, flue, and beazled."

"Goody Tumtops is usually right," I replied. "What happened? Are ye alright? I saw the airships over the mush, from St Mary's. Searchlights and Gatling guns."

"We'd just finished hauling the crop to the Tumtops farm when four Rozzer sky-sharks appeared. The Rozzers weren't after us, they were looking for these two. The chavvies came stumbling out of the wetlands, all cut about and tore, shivering and soaking wet. They're both prentices." Nellie nodded at the boy. "Pip's a Chopback. Liss here a Fishgut. Their sky-skiffs were ambushed over the Channel, then pursued and brought down over the salts. The chavvies are the only survivors, they saw the rest of the crews butchered in front of them."

"Not the usual Rozzer method."

"Liss said she bain't never seen em afore, she's convinced they weren't Coastguard or Royal Aero Fleet."

"Ye used to parley my ears off, when ye were…eleven?"

"She's twelve."

"Zackly, and it didn't always make sense, to be honest."

"One of the skiffs had a Wind Reader on board," Nellie said. "It'd be a poor prentice who did not heed the words of a Wind Reader. The chavvies talk like Free Traders. Liss can read the Owler's Script, I tested her. In fact, somewhen she parlays like a regular little Owling chief, and I reckon she's as stubborn as a chief, surely."

She gave me a pointed look and I grinned feebly in response. "I bain't stubborn."

Nellie rolled her eyes. "The girl be a proper little wildcat. She was about to tackle McFeck and his great big Scottish sword with her hatpin. A hatpin! Goody Tumtops threatened them with her broom to stop the two of 'em coming to blows."

"McFeck just now told me they were brave."

"No matter their age. Ye said ye saw the ships, Mum. So did I. They weren't chavvie inventions and they look like they spell moil for honest Free Traders. These chavvies are the only ones we know who got up close and personal with these particular Rozzers. I reckoned that mayhap ye'd be wanting to parlay with 'em. See what they can learn us."

I nodded approvingly. Part of Nellie's decision had been wise, the children might have useful information and there were

Rozzers out there machine-gunning peaceable Owlers minding their own business. "We'll have to find out what those Rozzer airships are," I conceded. "Howsumever, the chavvies be strangers. Why bring em here?"

"Zackly what I said," the maid muttered. "Why can't Hastings and Rottingdean look after their own? We got enough trouble as it is taking care of our own poor folk, without all of these furriners from faraway places turning up as strays and scrounging off us."

Nellie looked at her sternly. "Being the pious church-goer ye are, Breksid, I would have expected ye to be familiar with what the Good Book has to say about charity."

Breksid snorted, then resumed treating the boy's injuries. She did so tenderly enough, her grumpiness a permanent characteristic it seemed.

"The Mairemaid is our base," I pointed out. "There are other safe places, more secluded ones."

"I like 'em." Nellie shrugged. "They're bettermost chavvies…the girl, Liss. There's something about her, something special. We connected like we've known each other forever and longer. Mayhap it won't hurt me to forge friendships along the coast.

"Bettermost to trust naun at all," I said, although I knew Nellie had formed her own opinion on that matter.

"Zackly, jess so," Breksid muttered.

"Asides," my voice took on a lighter note. "Weren't ye busy enow 'forging' friendship with Sam from the Old Bell?"

Nellie blushed.

"Can't trust them Bell-Ends from the Old Bell," Breksid advised. "They got their end of town, we got ours."

I relented. If I wanted Nellie to run the Mairemaid and the Mudlarks someday, that involved allowing her to grow into the role by taking decisions. If I ordered the chavvies to be moved now, all would know I had countermanded Nellie's instructions

Nellie gently rolled the girl onto her back, tutting at the lacerations that criss-crossed the girl's limbs.

I stared at the girl's face, frozen to the spot, forgetting to breathe for a moment.

Scylla
Kill it.

Tess

It couldn't be. There were myriad explanations, perfectly logical, to suggest I might easily be wrong. Yet I knew I wasn't. I knew beyond any doubt who this child was.

 "Kill it," Scylla said once again, with a vengeful conviction that told me she wasn't speaking in jest as she sometimes does about these matters.

I shook my head.

"Then take it outside," Scylla advised. "The both of them. Boot them out of the inn. Send them back to the marshes. Let the Sky Gods decide their fate and there won't be blood on your hands."

"I won't," I said softly.

"How often have you secretly dreamed of having such power?" Scylla asked, rhetorically because she and I knew the answer fully well. "Kill it."

"I won't do that," I answered more firmly.

"Mum?" Nellie looked at me with concern in her eyes and voice. "Who are you talking to?"

I stared at her with consternation, before I muttered "nobody" and then fled the Blue Room.

I stopped briefly by the taproom, to establish all was well. The bar staff were coping with the extra business. As I had hoped, the ale, gin, and Brandywine flowed in copious quantities.

The band had just ended a song. Duke Box walked to the front, infectious joy shining on his face. "Ladies and Gents. Marsh Folk and Furriners. Let's welcome to the stage, all the way from the Garish Theatre in Lichfield…"

Three people stepped forward, two men and a woman, all three dressed as gentry. The woman wore a long black skirt, but other than that her attire was masculine, including black coat, black waistcoat, a paisley shirt, old fashioned cravat rather than a bow tie, and top hat. Her dark hair was done up in twin coils that curved along in perfect alignment with the curl of the brim of her hat.

"Here to entertain you," Duke Box continued with an elaborate flourish of his arm. "Johnny Moonstruck, Charles Wainright, and none other than the indomitable Joyce Jameson!"

Like I've said before, Sinneport is isolated and we're less likely to know the ins and outs of popular entertainment, but to judge by the enthusiasm with which the announcement was greeted, some of our marsh folk had heard of this lot before.

"Thank you, thank you," Joyce Jameson spoke with a gracious smile. "We'd like to perform 'Burlington Belles.'"

This was greeted by more cheers as the musicians started a new tune and the theatre folk began to sing.

Oh for the love of it
Oh for the hate of it
Oh for the "Damn, nearly getting away with it"
Oh for the sighing and rueing the day of it
Oh for those Belles.

Confident that the taproom didn't require immediate attention, I strode away through the panelled corridor that led deeper into the inn, the voices of the Lichfield group still audible.

Ain't that always the way of it
Oh My! Oh I was taken in!
(Oh, all my eye and that Betty Martin!)
A man must acknowledge the wages of sin

And not blame those Belles for the mess that he's in!

I made my way down the stairs, into the cellars, needing some time alone, to think, to contemplate the wages of sin the Lichfield group sang about with such cheerful jollity.

There was a small room behind the central chamber, where Nellie and I kept our Free Trader disguises. Nellie was wearing the Neeva outfit still, but my things…

Scylla
…our things...

Tess
…were there, adorning a mannequin fashioned from interwoven willow reeds.

Unlike the dark cloaks and clothing worn by the Mudlarks, this outfit was magnificent and elaborate. The dress wasn't practical and not worn out on runs, rather, it was designed to impose and impress. Accompanying it was a wig in the form of sea weeds cascading down, and an elegant masquerade mask in the shape of a skull.

This was the outfit of Scylla, the Mairemaid of Sinneport. Mothers all along the coast, from Chichester to Folkestone, warned their children to be good or else Scylla and her Mudlarks would come to fetch them and drag them kicking and screaming into the marshlands. Free Traders along the coast spoke her name in hushed, reverent tones, emphasising that the Mairemaid of Sinneport was not to be crossed.

Of late, Nellie had worn the disguise too, leaving me free to observe from the side lines dressed as Neeva. It was a useful extra layer of disguise, and a gambit we hadn't shared with anyone else. I suspected that Pug, McFeck, and my other old Parsevals weren't fooled by it, but I knew I could rely on their discretion.

I was aware of subtle differences, of course, in Scylla the Mairemaid's performances. Nellie and I were of a similar build and she had studied my mannerisms well. Voice wasn't an issue, because Scylla's costume had a voice distorter that transformed our voices into a mechanical rasp, meaning the slight differences in our tone and intonation made no difference. It was only disguised as Neeva that we had to mind our voices.

The crucial giveaway, as far as I was concerned, were the words spoken that revealed underlying thoughts. My Free Trader daughter was good at playacting ruthlessness when required, but she lacked the steeled, cold-blooded killer instinct required by my former trade.

I stared at the skull mask. The empty eye sockets stared back.

Scylla
The girl.

Tess
Like a ghost of sorts, truly the dead walk among us this night. I hadn't wanted my memories to run their full course. Had I not paid my dues, relived my pains with pounding headaches and helpless rage? Must I relive my mistakes for evermore?

Some six years after my purchase of the Mairemaid, six years of watching Nellie grow into a lively little girl, and six years of working hard to establish the Mudlarks as Free Traders to be reckoned with, I overheard a conversation between Brighton fishermen who had hastily set their hogboats on a course to Sinneport to avoid coarse weather.

From their words I gathered that Hawkeye too had returned to England, no longer a privateer but chief now of the Rottingdean Free Traders and making a name for himself.

My first reaction had been scorn. Too good for a pirate's life, Hawkeye hadn't objected to Free Trading? That had turned into quiet satisfaction that we were both trying our hands at the same profession.

As I gleaned more information about Hawkeye's new career and growing reputation, a tiny seed of hope was planted in my mind, or was it my heart? Regardless, I came to think, I persuaded myself, that we may not have matched as pirate and privateer, but hadn't we both started anew on equal footing as Free Traders?

Scylla objected, fought me tooth and nail, and did what she could to extinguish my hope to lay eyes on Hawkeye again. To no avail, the notion had taken root, grew into longing, and then a driving desire.

Why not? We had been so good together, so right together in all other respects.

I made a momentous decision, which I deemed to be a generous gesture on my part. I decided to forgive Hawkeye. Forgive and forget.

Still, many months passed before I gathered enough courage to journey west. First to Brighton, where I behaved most uncharacteristically by shopping for clothes and having my hair done, wanting Hawkeye to be as astonished as possible when we met again. I did not send word, and doubted he knew I too was in Sussex again, as my own reputation as Free Trader was based on Scylla's name and Scylla he knew not.

How naïvely excited I had been when I travelled on to Rottingdean. Exhilarated, lost in girlish dreams about our impending reunion, the laughter and delight when he'd sweep me up in his arms, but also thrilled by more base desires.

The gods love irony. The bloody cruel bastards must have had a right laugh at my expense that day, the worst possible day I could have picked to visit the small fishing village.

I saw my Hawkeye again, just as I had fervently wished for. Arm-in-arm with his glowing bride as they departed the church, both their faces delirious with happiness, the church bells ringing joyously.

He saw me not. When his head began to turn my way, an unexpected and uninvited late guest to his wedding, I ducked behind a large row of gravestones, trying to breathe, just about the most complex task I could tackle in that stunned moment.

I returned to Sinneport an empty shell, thunderstruck and devoid of emotions as I dared not let them near. I spent months in grief, torn between the pain of a heart once again ripped asunder, and sheer hatred which I directed at Hawkeye, his bride, but most of all myself. How utterly stupid and foolish I'd been.

It was in those days that Scylla effectively ran the business, coming to the fore like never before, and I let her, grateful to be granted space to nurse my wounds.

I never saw Hawkeye again. He was killed by Rozzers a few years ago. They had ambushed him returning from a run over the Channel. Having convinced myself I hated the man with every fibre of my being, I didn't grieve. However, considering the amount of times I had wished him dead, slowly and painfully so, I felt no satisfaction either, just numbing emptiness that was an echo of my pitiful state after visiting Rottingdean.

I had only seen the brabagious draggle-tail that Hawkeye married just the once, but her face was burned into my memory. In due course I learned her name: Clara Gunn from Brighton, as well as finding out they'd had a daughter.

A daughter who, I now knew, was a spitting image of her mother.

<u>**Scylla**</u>
Kill it.

<u>**Tess**</u>
Nellie's voice, her words replayed in my mind. "Like we've known each other forever and longer."

Our daughters have become friends?

Could I let that happen? Risk the one thing I was truly proud of in life, the one person who I loved unconditionally, by exposing yet another Hawkhurst to a Hawkeye?

Perhaps my mind was playing tricks on me. All Hallow's Eve. Old memories and regrets conjured up by tonight's music. The tendency of older age to dwell in the past and amplify nostalgia.

It could be pure coincidence that the girl in the Blue Room was from Rottingdean. More folk lived there than just Hawkeye's draggle-tail and their brat. And wasn't anything other than that simply too coincidental to even be real?

I had to know for sure. Before I did anything rash, foolish…or wise.

I took a last look at Scylla's outfit. Regal, befitting a smuggling queen, a disguise which had become so more than just that.

I went back upstairs, slowly, my body aching from tension. I felt old beyond my years. Force of habit drove me to the taproom first, to hear the close of a song about Lye Street.

Duke Box followed with another elaborate introduction as if he were welcoming royalty. "Come here tonight from Brighton, ladies and gents, misfits and miscreants, please give a hearty welcome to…Mishkin!"

A woman made her way to the fore of the group of musicians. She had compelling eyes, short bright red hair that barely reached her shoulders, and a face that was young still yet seemed haunted by too much knowledge of life's hardships. Her presence was enough to hush the taproom into a silence, laden with anticipation.

The musicians began to play, drums and guitars launching into a tune that caused goose bumps to tickle my arms and legs. It was a sound I'd never expected to hear in the Mairemaid. It was a sound that transported me thousands of miles and many years away: The distinctive rhythm of a tangomão tune.

Mishkin began to sing, her voice one of raw emotive power.

The road to ruin is paved
With the backs of the brave
And all the pretty things they said
I myself walked that path
And indeed surpassed
All the stupid limits I set
But if I only knew then what I still don't know now,
Would I plough on ahead, or turn it around?

I stood rooted to the spot for a moment, torn between my desire to rush upstairs to determine the truth of this mysterious girl…

<u>**Scylla**</u>

…and kill it…

<u>**Tess**</u>

…and an insane urge to move closer to the musicians and dance with a ghost.

Would I pick myself up
From my deep pile rug
And realise one day,
Enough is never enough.

The lyrics were too close for comfort and I fled the taproom, nearly bumping into Nellie and Sam in the panelled hall. Nellie was back in her regular dress, face hastily wiped clean of face paint. The two young people were entirely oblivious to my presence, locked in a tight embrace, eyes shut, and lips welded together.

I ignored them and rushed on, the distinctive tangomão rhythm and Mishkin's voice seeming to follow me with dogged persistence.

The wages of sin, it's a bottle of gin
And memories you'd rather forget.
It's growing old alone, so bitter, so cold
Add ice, lemon, and regret.

Pug had taken McFeck's place by the door of the Blue Room, seated on a chair, pistol on his lap. The tattered garments were gone. Pug saluted me with his hook but said nothing as I entered the room and closed the door behind me again.

The room was quiet, dimly lit by a candle left burning in its holder on the dresser. The children were asleep, but the girl at least, must have been awake, for her bed was empty. She had climbed into the boy's bed, and the two had snuggled into an innocent embrace, fast asleep.

I picked up the candle and walked to the bed slowly, hesitantly, fearing the girl would wake and not knowing if she'd open her eyes to see my confusion or Scylla's vengeful countenance.

If looks could kill, Scylla would have probably murdered us all at that moment without a moment's thought. She stared at me with icy disdain and contempt, thinking me weak.

She had never forgiven me for wrestling back control after I had emerged from my Rottingdean stupor. She'd done a good job but would have run the Mairemaid and the Mudlarks into the ground in the long run, never able to think like an innkeep or Free Trader, it was the pirate's life for her until the end. I had drawn the line at keelhauling captured Rozzers, it would only have escalated tensions in Romney Marsh.

I sat down on the bedside, searching the girl's face. The resemblance between this Liss and her mother was stronger even than that between Nellie and I, but I could see hints of Hawkeye as well.

So it was her. The daughter of my nemesis, who was probably unaware of my existence, but who had stolen Hawkeye's heart from me nonetheless. Hawkeye's little girl. Here in the lion's den, unprotected and in my power.

I reached out a trembling hand, then quickly drew it back when I sensed Scylla tried to take control of my hand, beginning to form a claw.

Clutching my hands together, I sat there, looking at the children.

The Blue Room was located close to the taproom, and I could hear Mishkin continue to sing below.

Older now, but still not the sow
You predicted upon our retreat
Oh, and how many times has my vengeful mind,
Had your head on a plate by my feet.

<u>Scylla</u>

His head on a plate. Don't deny it. You yearned for it. We yearned for it.

And now, now we have something Hawkeye would have considered far more precious than his own head. You know what he was like, this little girl would have been his treasure, the gleaming gold bullion of his eye.

They nearly crushed you, Tess my dear. Would you have pulled through if I hadn't been there? They came so close to breaking you entirely, and now, now it's payback time.

Send her severed head back to Rottingdean so all may know that neither El Escorpion nor Scylla the Mairemaid of Sinneport should ever be crossed.

You dreamt of revenge. It is yours to take. You earned it. Do it. Do it now.

Tess

It was a frozen scene of serenity, yet also a battleground. I had never fought such a dreadful battle as this one before. Scylla alternated between raining down her scorn on me, pleading for vengeance, and demanding the girl be killed.

I persisted in not heeding her torrent of angry words and ferocious emotions.

Waging war against children wasn't the pirate's way, nor the Free Trader's way, nor did I want to make it my own way. I stared hard at the children as I tried to shut Scylla out.

They looked so peaceful, so young still. The way they clung on to each other was endearing, scared no doubt after seeing their crews die in front of their eyes and running through the marsh for their lives; frightened, alone, and far away from home.

My mind jumped from the innocent embrace in front of my eyes, to the far less innocent business Nellie had been up to with Sam when I swept past them in the corridor, to languid tropical embraces with Hawkeye, and then the raging ruin I'd been left in.

Some of those experiences no doubt awaited these two, their current innocence replaced by instinctive curiosity, and then that headlong rush to experience the joys and delights that always held the danger of turning sour. Ever on it went, these inevitable circles, the turning wheel of fortune, the replays of human nature. The mere thought of it all was exhausting.

But if I only knew then what I still don't know now
What could I do? Change?
No diamond or dream, sovereign or bean
Could buy back even one of those days.

I recalled what the Wise Woman had said in the taproom.

While there are green leaves on the trees, something of summer remains. When the last leaves have gone, winter has come.

My winter was starting, even though I'd been resisting it. Perhaps it was time to accept it and live it in the peaceful serenity I'd once imagined I longed for.

Yes, I could have taken my revenge and shattered the life of Clara Gunn in the same way she had once unwittingly reduced mine to dark nothingness. But in doing so I'd terminate the future of this young girl and be destroying Nellie's reputation, for she had taken this young girl under her protection.

Hospitality, once extended, was sacred. Must children suffer for their parents' sins?

Once again, I extended my hand. It wasn't trembling this time as I softly stroked the girl's forehead.

She shifted slightly in response, and without waking mumbled: "Mum?"

I fought back an overwhelming wave of sadness. "No, my dear," I said softly. "But I could have been."

That realisation, that admission, sent Scylla reeling into a retreat, screaming shrilly but ineffectually.

"And I wish I had been, sweetheart," I added.

But if I only knew then, what I still don't know now,
I'd rather had nothing than live without.
So here's to us my dear, and here's to the past
And to think they said, you and I'd never last.

I bent over and kissed the girl's forehead. A tear fell from my eye onto her cheek, and I gently wiped it away.

When I straightened, I felt a hand on my shoulder. Nellie had entered the room with Free Trader's silent tread and joined me.

"Shouldn't ye be driving yer young man wild?" I asked Nellie. "Sam bain't half the man I think he is, if he bain't willing to abide patiently when I'm worried about my mum."

I smiled, raised my hand to my shoulder to lay it upon hers and squeeze it lightly. "Bethanks, but I'm alright now."

I looked around. Scylla was gone. Entirely. It was over. Inside, a bittersweet mix of relief but also regret because I knew I would miss she who had been my constant companion for so many years.

I rose to my feet, the burden of age less painful now. "Come, those damned musicians will be finished soon, we ought to be in the taproom when they do."

The wages of sin, it's a bottle of gin
And memories you'd rather forget
It's growing old alone, so bitter, so cold.
Add ice, lemon, and regret.

Nellie went to the bar when we reached the taproom and brought me a gin.

"With lemon and ice," she said. "Howsumever, I'm afraid we've plain run out of regret."

I laughed. "Don't worry, I have enow for all. This round is on me."

I looked at the ceiling, in the direction of the room where the children slept – safely, under my protection. I'd set out extra guards tonight, just in case Rozzers were still looking for her. I'd help the girl get back home, back to her mother, and Clara Gunn would never know what that cost me, but perhaps Hawkeye, wherever he was, would see…and know.

The logs in the fire shifted, sending sparks rising up into the chimney. I raised my glass to the hearth in silent toast.

Here's to us, my dear, and here's to the past. To think they said you and I would never last.

Ye Sky Gods, but three times lucky I suppose, Hawkeye and Hawkhurst allied again, a new hawkish venture.

The music had come to an end. Grizzly-man, Prospector, and Sailor approached me, expectancy on their faces.

I stared at them balefully for a moment. There was a great deal of understanding in their eyes, suggesting their arrival at the Mairemaid wasn't coincidental. Had they been grinning, their eyes triumphant at the outcome of their shenanigans, I might have been tempted to favour a retaliation of sorts. However, the understanding in their eyes was accompanied only by genuine respect.

Sighing, I admitted, "Ye moved me. Ye'll receive double pay on the morn. Howsumever…"

"There's always a 'but', isn't there?" Sailor asked the others.

"Two, as a matter of fact," I told him. "The first is that ye leave on the morrow and never come back."

"As you wish," Grizzly-man said. "Our work here is done."

"The second?" Prospector asked.

"Play me a few more songs," I said. "Please. I feel like dancing."

"That we can do!" Grizzly-man grinned. "Any preferences?"

"Do you know more tangomão?" I asked hopefully.

"Aye-aye, Cap'n," Sailor brought his knuckles to the rim of his tricorne.

I smiled, then looked at Nellie, stretching out my hand. "Come on, Dear, I've got a few things to learn you yet."

**THE
END**

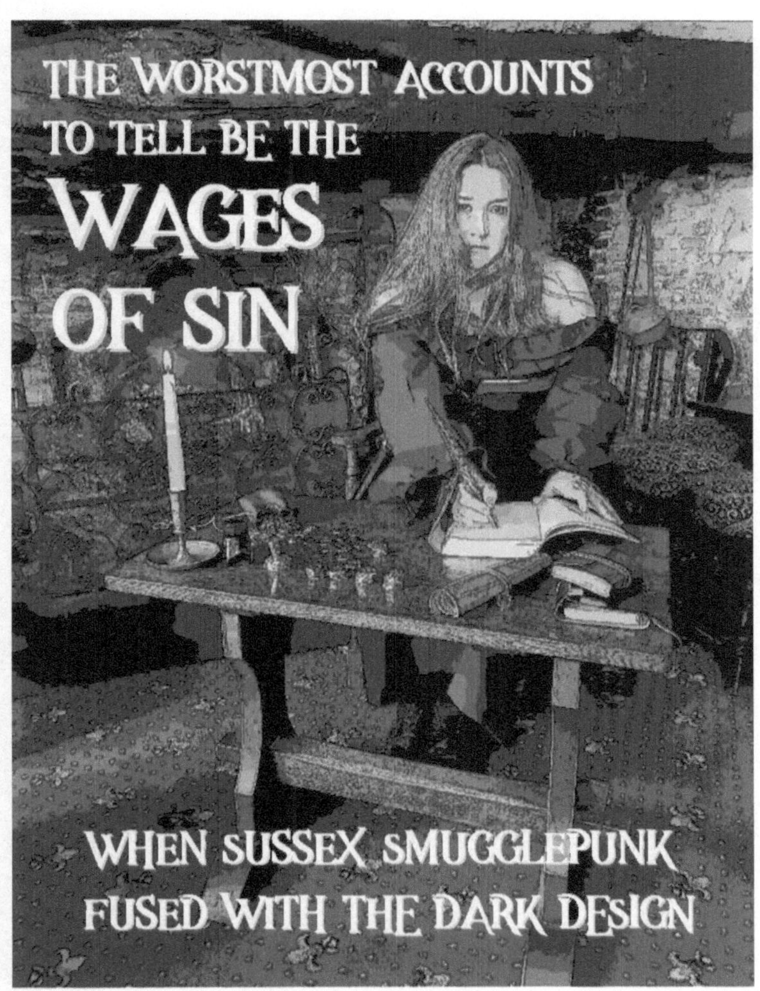
THE WORSTMOST ACCOUNTS
TO TELL BE THE
WAGES
OF SIN
WHEN SUSSEX SMUGGLEPUNK
FUSED WITH THE DARK DESIGN

ABOUT THE AUTHOR & CONTRIBUTING FRIENDS

Told once too often that he spends too much time in his imagination, **Nils Nisse Visser** moved there on a permanent basis, having located it in Brighton, Sussex. He's embarked on a rather insane quest to retell old Sussex folklore (and some Dutch sealore) within the genre of historical fantasy, including Smugglepunk (his own take on Steampunk). Entering his fifties, Visser hopes to become a pirate when he grows up.

www.nilsnissevisser.co.uk

Penny Blake comes from a storytelling background and writes Steampunk and Mythpunk inspired by her Rromani and Celtic heritage.

www.blakeandwight.com

Nimue Brown writes poetry, magazine articles, newsletters, mumming plays, short stories, flash fiction, songs, odd little cartoons about drama llamas, non-fiction books about Paganism, and speculative novels. Some of this is because she has a low boredom threshold, and some of it is because she is far too easily persuaded...

She also writes and colours for the graphic novel series Hopeless Maine, and its various tentacular offshoots. Aside from the short story in this collection, there is also a Hopeless Maine role play game, two illustrated prose novels, assorted music and performance material, and a community site where people who want to play with the island, do so.

The Hopeless Maine blog –
www.hopelessvendetta.wordpress.com

Duke Box is a fictional Steampunk character and promoter of Steampunk community events, as well as singer in The Wandering Wurlitzer. What is a Steampunk Gent? A host, a presenter, a master of ceremony, a thrower of parties, a compare, a rabble rouser, a raconteur, a filler in between acts, a parlour games inventor and instigator.

https://www.facebook.com/Steampunkgent/
dukebox.steampunkgent@gmail.com

Corin Spinks

The interior cover image has been created by photographer Corin Spinks. Tess Hawkhurst is kindly modelled by Lara Blair from Shimmy Armageddon & The Boxes of Chaos Performance Troupe.

www.facebook.com/corin.spinks
www.flickr.com/corinography
www.youpic.com/photographer/Corinography/

About the story

The story 'Wages of Sin' takes place on an evening that crosses the path of the novel *Fair Night for Foul Folk*, which recounts a smuggling run gone bad from the perspective of Alice Kittyhawk, the young Hawkeye from this story. This includes Alice's short stay at the Mairemaid Inn (Mermaid Inn) of Sinneport (Rye), and encounter with Tess, Scylla, Neeva, and Nellie.

Both 'Wages of Sin' and *Fair Night for Foul Folk* can be read separately from each other but reading both will reveal satisfying overlap.

The visitors from the Garish Theatre in Lichfield, namely Joyce Jameson, Johnny Moonstruck, and Charles Wainright are minor characters from Penny Blake's novel The Curious Adventures Of Smith and Skarry.

The introductory words on Samhain/All Hallow's Eve have been gathered from various blogs written by Nimue Brown. Duke Box is greatly thanked for supporting the anthology, writing his own main introduction within the story, but also kindly composing an introductory verse which we've worked into a photo-comic format.

In his Captain Pugwash and the Great Reward, John Ryan called Rye 'Sinkport', as a wordplay on Cinque Ports, the medieval confederation of south-eastern ports of which Rye was a part. I've changed Sinkport to Sinneport to also allude to Russel Thorndyke's Dr Syn and his Romney Marsh smugglers, and by happy coincidence or fateweavers' design, it also ties into the title of the song Wages of Sin by The Dark Design.

The Mermaid Inn was named the Barmaid Inn by Ryan. 'Mairemaid' is an approximation of how 'mermaid' was pronounced in 19th century Rye. The Mermaid Inn dates to medieval times. It was visited by William Shakespeare and The Lord Chamberlain's Men, who likely performed Love's Labour's Lost there. In later years it was frequented by members of the infamous Hawkhurst Gang, who drank and boasted with their guns and cutlasses openly on the tables.

I am grateful to Judith Blincow of the Mermaid Inn for granting us an opportunity to recreate the Hawkhurst gang scenes in her taproom in the company of assorted misfits.

All images by Yuliya Nazaryan, licensed by Dreamstime.

FEATURED SONGS

Bell Bottom Trousers – A huge 19th century music hall hit.

Smuggler – Traditional Scottish, adapted by author.

Smuggler's Daughter – Traditional, adapted by author.

Blow the Man Down – Shanty, traditional.

Samhain Song – written by Nimue Brown, used with kind permission.

Oh My Love is Gone – Traditional Sussex, minor adaptions by author.

Burlington Belles – Chorus from a music hall song written by Penny Blake for The Curious Adventures Of Smith And Skarry, used with kind permission.

Wages of Sin – By The Dark Design, sung by Mishkin Fitzgerald on the 12 Tall Tales album.

LYRICS: LYE STREET

INTRO

The Messages Continued to Haunt Carnival. She found no escape from them. In every Dark Attic and abandoned hovel, they cried out to her from the walls...LYE Street LYE Street...Lye Street...Go to the Lye Tower...The Moon thinned as the penultimate Scar Night of the year drew near. She could feel the blood quickening in her veins and the hunger reaching up and curling around her like ivy. Her time to hunt was close.

SONG LYRICS

The truth lies in Lye Street,
But lies linger there too...
Keep your wits with you,
As you wander through,
The maze is always waiting,
So you better you choose a path...
Careful what you wish for and be careful who you ask...

We all have one beginning and all have one end...
And what matters in this life
Is what we do between them...

Hope lives in Lye Street,
But doubt dwells there as well,
One man's heaven is his brother's hell
So choose your direction,
Because you can't choose your friends,

Be careful what you wish for,
You might succeed in the end.

I lived on Lye Street,
Or at least I did once,
But the future was uncertain,
So forgive me I ran...
You see I've seen the future,
And I know how this ends,
Be careful what you wish for
And beware of your friends...

LYRICS: THE TALE OF THE RED QUEEN

INTRO

I do not fear the crossroads in life, to the contrary I seek them out. But I'd be a fool if I said I own no regrets, and it was just such a crossroad that I rue most in life. It was there at that dark junction where my story begins. Mars? Why in God's name did I agree to go to Mars? The answer is as clear today, as it was back then...for I can still hear her call...Come...come to me my love...

SONG LYRICS

This is the tale of the Red Queen...
Or maybe it was all just an opium dream...
I can pretend it didn't happen if you think that will help...
I can't tell you exactly how we got there
But I'll tell why we went...
For King and Country the letter said...
Determine the threat of invasion
And if needs be prevent it...
But our mission to Mars was doomed from the start...
Twelve months of planning, but it still fell apart...
The letter was itself curt...
Go to the red planet and neutralise the threat...
A service to the Empire... which we'll never forget...
Well that was a lie if nothing else...
I don't suppose we really had much of a choice...
But all I remember is death...
and death had such a beautiful voice...

She said, Come,
Come to Me My Love…
Come to Me My Love…
She said,
Come to me, Come
Come to Me My Love…

It was January 1893
When I met the nine others who would travel with me…
There were ten of us at the journey's start…
But I'm the only one of us that made it back…
Death was with us before we left…
It was almost as if our enemy lacked patience…
Jones went mad in the cold dark void
And before he shot himself,
He shot Smith and stabbed Jonny boy…
Cole's cabin burned up on entry,
I reached for the extinguisher but found it empty…
Foley's harness failed just as we landed
But despite brave attempts, he could not be revived…
Ten of us had set out for the surface of Mars
Which only five of us lived long enough to stand upon.
And all the while I heard that voice…

She said, Come,
Come to Me My love…
She said,
Come to Me My Love…
She said,
Come to Me, Come…

Come to Me My Love…

I'd expected rocks, I'd expected dust,
I hadn't really expected much,
But I never imagined that I would see a scarlet palace
On the shores of a crimson sea…
We buried our dead, sang 'God save the King'
And then made our way to the palisade…
If I knew then what I know now
There would be four more men with me right now…
As we approached from the southern shore
We crossed a rusty drawbridge over a ruby moat…
There were no guards on the battlements
The castle looked completely defenceless…
But that's just what she had intended…
And the voice grew ever closer…

She said, Come,
She said, Come
Come to Me My love…
Come
Come to Me My Love…
She said, Come to Me
Come to Me My Love…

And there on a throne made of souls
Was the Martian queen in a robe of bone…
Voices in my head said, 'strangle McCabe'
And I saw her smile as I turned to my friend…
As I reached out to grab his neck,
I saw Tommy Vines do the same to Nick…

Old Doctor Jones tried to escape
But the Martian queen, she wasn't finished yet...
Life faded from my friend and he went blue

I turned back to Tommy and he was finished too...
The Red Queen had given old Bill a knife
And in return for that he'd given her his own life.
In the end it was just Tommy and I,
And we both knew one of us had to die...
I knew then it wouldn't be me...
Because only the winner would get the Martian Queen...
As I knelt before her with Tommy's head on my lap,
She smiled, she winked, and then she clapped...
It was more than I had ever hoped
But then she opened her scarlet lips and spoke...

Your planet has nothing to fear
For I am just a prisoner here ...
I can never leave these walls
Let alone launch an assault?
But I greatly admire your desire
And by feeding on them I survive
And you brought enough here to me
To last a hundred years
But a girl's got to eat
And soon I'll be needing fresher meat
So I'm sending you home
So you can tell others to come...

Come to me My Love...
Come to Me, Come

Come to Me My Love
Come to Me My Love...
Come
Come to Me My Love...

Come to Me My Love...

THE TALE OF
THE RED QUEEN
Neil Campbell

THE TALE OF THE RED QUEEN
BY NEIL CAMPBELL

This is the tale of the Red Queen...
Or maybe it was all just an opium dream...
I can pretend it didn't happen if you think that will help...
I can't tell you exactly how we got there
But I'll tell why we went...

I bit Caruthers. They'll have to do it now. Three taps with Thompson's hammers and I'll be free. In honesty, I thought it would be easier than this. An ounce of delirium, add a pinch of night terror and a good old glug of faecal flinging and I was certain they would have had me hard strapped on the first stretcher to B wing before the end of the first night shift, but as with most of my damned life there's a problem. Nurse Dietmar Bloech believes me.

I'm not surprised, not truly. Conviction is powerful friend and a fearsome foe. There are those with the gift to read it like tea leaves. I have that gift. It served me well in the Raj. Metcaffe the merciful they called me in the letters I received from the furthest corners of that sweaty annex. "Honourable Sir" they'd start, and the darkest deeds would follow, ravishment, buggery. The best that war brings out in the worst of us. I should have known better; I should have kept have my blasted mouth shut. Should have, could have, god alone knows why I didn't? I'd doubt my tale too, but then I had the pleasure of watching it unfold with my own dull eyes.

I've never been one to pause. I've a broad chest, covered in gold coins and ribbons that say I know how to make a quick call. I've saved and damned men on my whim and My Lady Empire has praised and doomed me by telegram, handshake and shallow courtesy. I do not fear the crossroads in life, to the contrary, I seek them out, but I'd be a fool if I said I own no regrets. It was just such a crossroad that I rue most in life and it was there at that dark junction that my story truly begins.

Congratulations were due, it told me. I was to return to London to begin the celebrations and then it mentioned a twelve-month leave.

I read and reread the telegram almost hourly as I made the month-long steamer trip back from India. I could have done the whole blat by air in a week, but I have always considered myself a grounded sort and I despise the eerie feeling of flight. Besides, I was notorious among the Zeppelin Packets as a risky sort thanks to an infamous duel on the bridge of *The Nancy*.

Fifty-two weeks of thumb twiddling, gin drinking and whore baiting. They may as well have sentenced me to a year in Strangeways. I was not a man who did nothing well. I told myself on the trip that I'd make a proper nuisance of myself in the clubs of London and before they could blink, they'd have me back on the next steamer.

The journey itself was uneventful which only made my predicament worse. All play and no work makes Metcaffe a dull man indeed. Despite myself, I kept to my cabin for most of the last leg. I stuffed my pretty silver pipe with poppy powder and smoked like the ship itself. The sway of the sea was most agreeable and before I could say Straits of Gibraltar, I found myself on the prow of the ship staring up the muddy Thames towards the great rank plume of smoke that I knew to be London. I am fortunate never to have suffered the awful blight of sea sickness and despite the warnings of the liberal set I have never had so much as a head-ache from a pipe of opium, but I will confess I felt a little rum that morning as we chugged up the filthy estuary. Whatever the cause of my malaise, it most certainly contributed to my failure to spot the figure, who must have approached with canny stealth.

"I do wish sometimes there were warmer sights to welcome one back," he said.

It took me a moment to register that I had been addressed and another to respond.

"Yes," was all that I could muster, but despite my curtness, my new colleague clearly intended to chat.

"Travelled far?" He asked, I nodded and turned to face him with what I hoped was a withering glance.

"Colonel Metcaffe," he said, at once dropping the act, "I am not here by chance sir and clearly you are not a man of patience..."

I nodded but maintained my dagger-stare.

"So, who are you? And who sent you?"

"Imperial Defence sent me. My name is Lord Stephen Davies," he replied, and I realised before I turned to face the man that I already hated this Lord Stephen Davies.

"Well, Lord Stephen Davies," I said to his fine leather boots, "are we to chat about the weather before you get to the point? Let me guess, you'd like an after-dinner speaker at some treacherous members club? Or would you have a rogue platoon storm a diamond mine in Capetown? Or do the old boys at M.O.I.D. simply need someone to play conkers with the cloaks at M.I.6?"

"It's a matter of imperial security; I can't tell you anything here."

"Christ man, who here on the deserted prow of this bloody steamer is going to give the arse of a rat what nonsense your senile masters have concocted."

I summed him up then, gauged his reactions. There was a time in my life when I might have hurled him into the river for less than his mysterious nature and a shiver traversed the length of my backbone as I exorcised the thought that once I could have been so callous.

Lord Stephen Davies seemed to be making his own assumptions. A few seconds passed silently. Save for the thrum of the ship's great pistons and the sound of her wheels churning through the muck of the Thames, there was no other noise. We stood like that for, what felt like, a swift eternity. Then suddenly he spoke again.

"There are those within my office, who believe we are under threat of invasion."

"Her Majesty's Empire? Poppycock," I said. "There's not a country on earth with the might, manpower or technology to threaten our shores."

"I agree Colonel, but then I am just a messenger..." as he spoke, he knelt down and placed a leather satchel by my feet. "Inside you will find a hundred pounds and an invitation. I have done my duty Colonel Metcaffe, I can only hope you do yours."

To my disservice I didn't even deign to give the man a last glance and being in no mood for his cloak and dagger nonsense, I picked up the satchel he had laid at my feet and up ended its contents all over the steamer's quarter deck. My impatience cost me £10, if the stranger was telling the truth about the bag's contents and I see no profit in his dishonesty. It was not my rashness, but rather fate which scattered the satchel's cargo across the deck.

The breeze had been all too sudden and brief and before I could register what was happening, paper snowed all around me like a blizzard. I could discern charts and maps and obviously a number of bank notes amid the paper cyclone. Instinct kicked in and I set my dull muscles to work, ploughing first after the bank notes and then the charts, which were dancing out towards the sea and oblivion. I can't say I got them all and I'd like to say that perhaps if I had then I wouldn't have taken the assignment, but to my shame I failed to read even the scraps that I did save. All I could think about was the money I had squandered. I have never been a money man nor would I consider myself thrifty yet I, without the means to procure a room upon disembarkment had found someone who could. In turn, I shat on their charity like an ill-trained pet. In haste, I shoved the documents back into the satchel and in doing so I noticed that I had not emptied it. There inside, still intact, was a letter bearing the Imperial Seal.

When I found the initials M.O.I.D. on the envelope, I nearly turned the whole lot into the sea.

Don't get me wrong, I am no coward and my wanderlust and adventurous spirit have piqued the interest of scribblers the world over, but if there's one thing I cannot abide it's a bureaucrat. In my experience there was nowhere in the world so well wrapped in crimson tape as the Ministry of Imperial Defence. Still, I was in need of a brandy and since it was their round, I cracked the seal and sat down to read.

As I tried to read and reread the letter to myself, I became aware of the city appearing in the periphery. The sights, sounds and unfortunately the smell of the capital were overwhelming. The sky was littered with aircraft, some ornate, some others solid and vast, while the majority appeared to little more than cheap silk balloons and charcoal burners.

I took a deep breath and instantly regretted it. The air was thick with smoke, but even that wasn't invasive enough to spare me from the rank stench of effluence. I distracted myself by watching an approaching air liner. She had been shadowing the steamer for a couple of hours, using the ship's smokestack as a cheap thermal. It appeared she had grown tired of the tow and was making ready for her own approach to the city. She had doubled her speed during the minutes I'd watched her and would soon overtake the steamer.

I took a seat on a wrought iron bench at the ship's prow to watch the airship make her final approach. She was directly overhead and had dropped to barely 20 feet from our spinnaker. I could clearly make out her colours and her name plate. *The Delft* was a Dutch boat and had been built for those who liked a luxury. Her envelope looked lush as velvet and was the rich blue of midnight. She was a vision of teak and filigree gold.

As she passed overhead, she gunned her motors and her props roared in the morning air. I needed a hand to keep my hat and the impromptu blast scattered the few missing fragments of my satchel into the estuary.

She had nearly cleared our decks when I heard a shout above. In that moment she opened her cess tanks showering me in month old shit and piss.

The red mist descended, and I ran for my cabin and for revenge. I read the MOID letter over and over in my head as I made my way to my deck and a single thought escaped the confines of my furious mind. Time to see how powerful my new friends are...

It was a day later when the berserker rage subsided. I found myself in the dock of the Old Bailey being addressed by an old man in a wig and black silk gown, Richard Ryall he was called.

"Mr Metcaffe," Ryall said.

"Colonel Metcaffe," I corrected.

"Quite, Colonel Metcaffe, please explain again why and how you chose to shoot down a passenger Zeppelin over the Thames yesterday morning. A liner that was in fact ferrying the Crown Prince himself and bearing the colours of the Royal Dutch Trading Company, the airship commanded by none other than the famed Captain Karen Roberts."

I looked Ryall in the eye, and I did what my mother had always told me to do on such occasions, I lied.

"She was on fire." I said.

"Quite," Ryall said again. "Just so we are perfectly clear on this. Colonel, you ascertain that you fired on a vessel that you claim was on fire. Despite no evidence that anyone onboard had seen any sign of a blaze...let alone any smoke. Captain Roberts was very insistent this was not the case. Can you once again explain why you thought the appropriate and reasonable course of action was to shoot at it?"

"I reasoned that if they were unable to sense the danger of a fire aboard a hydrogen Zeppelin, then they might at least have sense enough to take care to avoid soiling their fine royal attire by plunging into the foul waters of the Thames."

"Are you actually telling this court that you risked the lives of every soul aboard *The Delft* in some insane attempt to save them?"

Ryall spoke at me, but not to me, it was evident he was addressing the twelve men good and true of the jury and his patronising tone was the last bag on the saddle.

"Have you ever seen a hydrogen fire? Or its effect?" I didn't wait for his reply. "It's quick."

I paused to ensure I'd snared the jury. Ryall opened his mouth to interrupt, but I silenced him with a wave and my best officer's voice. "One minute you're a proud husband with a fine dowry and pretty wife. Minutes later you're a man on the road to a slow death at the end of a gin bottle. I carried a man like that from the wreckage of *The Carpathian* after she went down in Istanbul. I carried him from the crash, but I couldn't save him. No more than I could save her, nothing can save you from those nightmares. I tried, and do you know the queerest thing?"

I paused again for effect and took my time to catch each and every pair of eyes in the jury. For good measure, I ensured that I established contact with Lord Howie, the judge, as well.

"It was the smell I remember most. My hair was gone and my whiskers, my clothes were alight and the pain was extraordinary. I still bear scars on my back that would curdle the stomach of battle-hardened surgeons, but it was the smell that I'll never forget. I've managed to suppress the screams. It's taken me ten years, but I'll never forget the smell, the sweet aroma of bacon as the hydrogen fires flash fried her two yards from my feet. They burned witches, indeed some say they still do in some corners of the Empire"

I halted again and scanned the faces astride the benches opposite. One could have heard a mouse fart in the silence, even Ryall and Lord Howie were absorbed by my tale. "They don't burn witches because it's cheap or quick, indeed it's quite the opposite, a good stoning or a drowning costs nothing. No, they burn them because burning to death is the most horrific thing on god's earth."

The barrister had strayed close to me, as if his proximity may have some leverage on my speech. I stole the opportunity to make a deeper point and if I'm honest to show him up a little.

"Nerves." I said, simultaneously striking at Ryall like a pit viper. I plucked a silver hair from the nape of his neck. He yelped like a terrier.

"Nerves," I repeated, addressing the jury this time. "Cover every inch of our bodies, thousands of them in just a pinch of skin. The hair I have just acquired from my learned friend struck but one of those nerves. When one burns to death, each and every nerve is fired. I'd rather be eaten by ants than burn to death and I assumed the passengers of *The Delft* would probably sooner have drowned. Not that drowning would be an option in the crowded estuary of the Thames, I mean for god's sake man I shot the bloody thing down from the deck of a damned steamer."

I paused again this time for no reason beyond malice.

"Are we really to assume our captain would have sailed by and watched her crew and passengers go under? This was not the doomed *The Northern Star*. These were no storm-weary sailors miles from the safety of shore. There was no hurricane and no harm done to the listening towers of the south bank. There were no harsh choices to be made aboard *The Delft*. Do not confuse these day trippers with the brave souls of *The Northern Star*. These nobles were not likely to die side by side with common ship hands, throwing their luggage and their treasures into the ocean to satisfy the angry gods of the sea and the storm. No, these fat, lazy bastards were so busy lounging and gorging, they had failed even to notice a bloody fire on their own ship. Captain Roberts, reputation notwithstanding, too busy no doubt fawning on royalty to mind her duties."

I could tell from the faces of the jury that I had done enough. There would be no conviction today. I still believe that, had they had the power, they might have decorated me for my bravery and quick wits. I was slightly concerned, however, for the lack of support my newfound friends at the Ministry had shown me. After all, it was in large part my new social circle that prompted me to shoot the Zeppelin from the sky. I scanned the galleries and whilst there was no shortage of people in the courtroom, none seemed the MOID sort. My eyes settled on Ryall who wore the look of man who'd been beaten but was going to fight on regardless. Part of me admired that in him. In my daze, I'd lost control of the room and my enemy didn't miss a beat.

"Colonel Metcaffe, can you explain what would happen if, just for arguments sake, you had shot at a Hydrogen Zeppelin which was not on fire?"

I was amazed he hadn't asked this question sooner.

"If I had been using a normal gun, albeit a very powerful one, I suppose I may have risked causing a hydrogen explosion," I said.

"A normal gun?"

"Yes, an elephant gun or an old blunderbuss, something large bore, a fire and forget affair."

"But your gun is not a normal gun?"

"Correct."

"Mr Metcaffe."

"Colonel..."

"Colonel Metcaffe, what kind of gun did you use to bring down the airship?"

I had been waiting for this question and I waited for him to repeat the question and then waited a few seconds more, for the moment in the room when true silence fell. I planned my moment well

"I used a spiritual oscillator."

The gasps in the room were audible. I may as well have told them I had used black magic, I fought hard to suppress a smirk. Ironic to think that my defence which had already alluded to the burning of witches could have easily had me condemned as one not forty years before

"I would like the court to know, that I for one, Colonel Metcaffe, do not believe a solitary word you have spoken this morning. In closing, I would also add that I believe you opened fire on an unarmed airship for no other reason than it happened to be there. And I find your use of Mr Mason's highly questionable weaponry to be in extremely poor taste, not to mention judgement, Guns powered by the dead? Disgusting, disgusting and ungodly."

Come to Me My Love.

"Believe what you will sir, I believe my case rests on the decision of my twelve peers behind you. I am most certain, that unlike you sir, they are free thinkers, not bound by the archaic statutes and scriptures of the last century. I am glad that I have their opinions to count upon. For if it were up to you sir, I feel I would soon be on a boat bound for some godforsaken colony and a life toiling in the cotton fields and all for the simple act of mercy."

I sneered at Ryall then, openly and in full view of the jury I spat at the floor in front of him. "Men like you make me sick."

It took the good jury under an hour to acquit me of all charges, and as I left the Old Bailey I wished I had spat on the QC rather than at his feet.

I was unsurprised to find a hackney blimp waiting on the wide avenue as I descended the stone steps of London's most famous courthouse. As I got closer, I was able to discern a figure in the frail gondola. They had sent a lady; I smiled, the MOID boys had done their homework. I never could refuse a pretty filly. As I approached the little airship, a man, who looked more boxer than butler, opened the gondola's saloon doors and I climbed aboard without a second thought. The young lady spoke the second my arse hit the wicker day bed.

"Pleased to meet you Mr Metcaffe. My name is Heather Rose Thorn." She spoke with a voice that I immediately thought I might very much like to hear again. I thought about correcting her, as I usually did when referred to in such a matey fashion, but I decided not to rock the gondola.

She pressed a large brass button on a central walnut console, and I heard the tell-tale whoosh of a burner and in seconds we were off. As we ascended over the city, she leant forward and placed a brazen hand on my knee before speaking again, once more in a warm and welcome tone. "Do try not to shoot this airship down Mr Metcaffe," she said. I don't know whether it was the location or her manner, but I was forced to stop myself flirting with the clearly capable Heather Rose Thorn.

Come to Me My Love

A thought drags me back to my cell and my future and what shreds of my mind I still retain. My once linear life is in rags and only my sheer bloody mindedness keeps me anywhere near sane.

Women, it was always women that steer me towards the rapids.

Dietmar wants to speak at my hearing and no amount of guessing could allow me to believe there was any other reason than the obvious… and that was bad news. Dietmar intends to speak on my behalf. Somehow, she has found a place in her heart for the truth, for some reason, she knows we'd been to Mars and therefore is prepared to accept what I had told her about our encounter.

Mars? Why in the hell did I tell her about the voyage. Hell, why the blazes did I agree to go?

Come to Me My Love.

"Mars?" I said. "You are mad."

The room was small and oppressive. I hadn't seen a single window on the entire floor and my instincts told me I was somewhere below sea level. I couldn't tell you exactly where or indeed how long it had taken us to get there. To be honest, I couldn't even tell you exactly where the blimp had landed. But I could tell you all about Miss Heather Rose Thorn. I'd never credited the Ministry of Imperial Defence with much in the way of intelligence, but after five minutes in the company of Miss Rose Thorn, I knew I had been quite mistaken. I'm loathed to admit it, but I'd probably have followed her all the way from India if she'd suggested the trip for a gas. The lady was delightful. As I mentioned, my memories of the gondola trip were few enough, but I could write a book about her. The exact shade of her auburn hair, the precise angle of the curve of her spine or the tone of her gentle laugh. If she had asked me to venture into the ninth level of hell to retrieve her pocketbook, I'd have gone without a word. By comparison, Mars seemed banal. She ignored my question and returned to her original plan of batting her doe eyelids and sitting uncomfortably close, but for all my righteous indignation, I couldn't stay angry at the delicate creature.

"It's a mission of the utmost importance," she said eventually. As she spoke I knew I was going, although I clearly remember being quite positive the journey, was in my opinion, beyond man or science.

"Alright, alright I will consider the request, but can you please explain why we have to go to Mars in the first place."

"Two thousand years ago, entire civilisations worshipped the planets and deities. To these cultures these heavenly bodies were in fact the gods themselves. Many were seen as symbols of love and harvest and other significant emotions and events, but one planet seems to have developed a universally more nefarious association."

"Mars," I said, picking up her thread.

"Mars is almost always associated with war. Let me tell you Mr. Metcaffe."

"Col..." I almost said, stopping myself just in time.

"The planet Mars is not merely associated with war. Many people actually believed it to be the God of War."

"I know my Latin, young lady."

"Apologies Colonel."

God she was good, I thought, noting her newfound accuracy. "Well, Colonel, the big wigs at the ministry are starting to think there was more than co-incidence at stake."

Enough was enough, she found my classical heel and I dug it in.

"You're serious!"

"Of course."

"Young lady there are parts of our planet we have yet to discover and MOID would have you believe we need to set off into the void to fight the Roman Gods? How are we to get there? In some kind of great iron spaceship?"

"You're mocking me, Mr Metcaffe."

Suddenly, I was back to plain old Mr Metcaffe.

"Well Ms Rose Thorn, how are we to face the God of War? Besides, it's a long way to Mars. I'd suggest we get moving."

"We already have Mr Metcaffe and I'm afraid you're in for the duration."

"Ah, we're travelling by make-believe. Excellent, may I have a Venusian gin and tonic? Oh, and a pair of Balinese dancers wouldn't go a miss while we're at it."

"Actually, we're travelling by Zeppelin, presently at least."

"Of course, we are my dear and we'll be there in what? Two thousand years?"

"Twelve months actually, if the winds hold and we don't miss our connection."

"Ah the 12:45 Martian Express from Stoke isn't it?"

"Our connection is a comet Mr Metcaffe, and if you miss it, you all die."

"Ms Rose Thorn, it's been a hoot, it really has, but I'm out of whisky and you are out of marbles, so if you wouldn't mind, I have a living to earn. Now do pass on my regards to MOID and tell them thanks for the hundred pounds, which will come in very handy on my return journey I'm sure." I set down my glass and raised a practised eyebrow at my companion.

She said nothing and I felt the urge to fill the silence.

"I really can't spare the time for a jaunt to outer space right now. So, if you be so kind to wire me a hackney blimp, I'll bid you good day."

I bowed and doffed my hat as I spoke, but by the time I raised my head Ms Heather Rose Thorn has released the roller blinds on a large window behind her and at the same time my grip on sanity.

I could see from the view that we were aloft and not just flying, but at altitude. Higher than I had ever been, and indeed higher than I had thought it possible to be.

"I felt no movement." I said, instantly realising I'd just spent an hour making a fool of her and she wasted no time in returning the favour.

"We have offset the inertia; the process will continue throughout the journey. You are going to Mars, Colonel Metcaffe. I'm sorry, but you never really had a choice. We don't have any Venusian Gin, but I believe I could find some Bombay, if you still want that drink. It will help with the next part of the process."

I nodded, and she continued as she made her way to a walnut bar and mixed some drinks.

"This Zeppelin is filled with a unique element, Mr Metcaffe, a gas unlike any other. It's as light as hydrogen, but with a lower flashpoint than oxygen. I can only tell you at this point, that every cubit of this gas that exists is in the envelope above us and that there is a five percent chance we will explode before we reach our destination."

"Five percent?" I asked, "I've won good money on longer shots than that."

She returned with a crystal glass filled to the brim with bitter Gin.

"Such is the price of our venture. Colonel, we have received incontrovertible proof that there is not only life on Mars, but there is intelligent life. We don't know who or what they are, but we believe they are plotting to invade."

I sipped gingerly at my drink as she spoke. Questions I should have asked earlier flooded my confused mind.

"You mentioned a connection something about a comet wasn't it? And the promise of certain death?"

"We haven't really got time for all the answers now and to be frank, I'm no expert, but I can tell you that we are approaching what the scientists tell me is a window. Other than that, I've told you all I know. We're approaching the muster point soon and the boffins can tell you more."

"There are others?"

"Oh Colonel, you are priceless; did you really think that MOID was sending the pair of us to deal with the threat of a Martian invasion alone? You may have been a hero in the Raj, but I doubt they expect you to fend off the invasion single handed."

I could feel all the jibes I'd made at her expense over the last hour or so ready to return, she was loving this. Suddenly a voice sounded from nowhere. Before I even registered what it had said I instinctively reached for my revolver and made a move to protect Ms Rose Thorn. It was then that I realised the voice had addressed me by name.

"Colonel Metcaffe?" the voice said again, it sounded like it had originated in the bottom of tin drum. Only then did I realise it expected an answer.

"Yes" I replied, trying to make my voice sound in as many directions as I could, completely unsure about where I should be projecting.

"Splendid," it said, "We can hear you loud and clear. You must have a hundred questions what would you like to know first?"

"What the devil is going on?" I blurted.

"We're off to give the Martians a sound thrashing. What else do you want to know?"

"How?" It was one word and all I could think of.

"Fine, fine I'll tell you. Let me know when I lose you."

"I'm not an idiot," I said.

"You're no quantum physicist either old boy, but we can't all be perfect. Ask yourself how far it is to Mars?"

"I've no idea? How far is it to Mars?"

"Ah you see you're asking the wrong question. What you should be asking is how far away Mars is today."

"Special occasion is it?"

"Not yet, but it will be. In twelve months, Mars and Earth will the closest they have been to each other in history, well at least for as long as we can calculate. Mars will be at its Perihelion and Earth at its aphelion. We have different orbits you see Colonel; oh, do let me call you Reg."

I nodded and a giggle from Ms Rose Thorn highlighted how ridiculous the gesture had been.

"There are two other factors to consider Reg, Ice and Wind."

"Ice and wind? You've lost me."

"Aha see, I said we would. Never mind, it was a trick question of sorts. I'm talking about Comets and Solar winds, Reggie. As we speak, the Comet Lovejoy is hurtling through our solar system, accelerated to record speed by the strongest solar wind ever. As luck would have it's going to miss Earth by approximately a thousand miles, before hurtling on to Mars which it might actually hit, or so the book tells us. Although I'll admit the book is staggering."

"Book?"

"Oh, top secret, it's a book of great power and we still don't understand it all."

"So, when does all this hurtling happen? And what's all this about certain death if we miss the connection?"

"Good questions, well, we've done the sums, but we're about to test a thousand theories and if any of them go wrong then we're back to the drawing board, and remember the nearest drawing board is five miles beneath us and the only thing hold you up is the most explosive substance known to man... and the only thing preventing it from exploding is em..."

"Theory?"

"Quite!"

It was at this point I knew my mind had gone full circle. It had begun with the assumption I was dealing with lunatics, briefly toyed with the idea they might in fact know what they were doing, before finally swinging back round to my initial findings. It was quite clear to me that I was about to die and therefore there was really only one thing to do. I held up my empty glass tapped it with my pinkie finger and gently coughed in the direction of the lovely Ms Rose Thorn.

I feel like a cheat, I can't tell you how we got there, I really can't. The logistics weren't my area. In the Raj I'd led men through the vilest hell and it seemed my new masters needed a man like that. It wasn't my job to get them to Mars; it was my job to keep them sane when they got there.

It was January 1893 when I met the nine others who would travel with me. There were ten of us at the journey's start, but I'm the only one of us that made it back, death it seems; was with us from the start.

Fragments, that's all I can tell you, uttered phrases, the odd term. I'm afraid to say I lacked even the basest interest in the mechanics of the journey. I can tell you about the gondola though, I'll never forget that.

They named her *The Red Queen*, an irony which will dawn on you, as it dawned on me.

She was some fantastic alloy, another boon from the great book that I would come to hear so much about.

As Ms Thorn led us across the gangplank from our Zeppelin to the gondola, she seemed to mention the book more and more. It truly seemed to be the all-powerful entity her colleague had told us about during our first meeting.

My life is littered with pivotal moments. Like the *Carpathian* disaster, the ten days we held the Khyber Pass, and the glow of the Southern Lights washing over the ballroom of *The Northern Star* as I swayed cheek to cheek with La Dutchessa as the bells broke 1880. Nothing, however, could compare to the nine feet I walked five miles over the Earth to climb aboard *The Red Queen*.

The thin walkway was made of finest teak and appeared wafer thin. Below, I could see the curve of the planet and more hues of blue that I believed existed, but despite the wonder of looking down on my home as only a god might, I could not tear my eyes from *The Red Queen*.

Her joints, her rivets, even her paint, all had their foundations in Ms Thorn's mysterious tome. She talked and talked about MOID's latest creation and despite her fervour for the vessel, I can only remember a single fact. She was a steamer, oh god...how could I forget that, a bloody interstellar steamer!

"*The Red Queen* will actually turn the Comet's ice to steam to set and alter course," she said, "although her real power will be inertia."

Ms Thorn spoke more about inertia, but gin had fogged the rest of the lecture. It was during that first tour that I met Foley.

Foley stood a head shorter than I, which to my mind made him five eight or in the neighbourhood. He sported wire frame spectacles with one lens a good inch thicker than the other. His skin seemed somehow thin and I found myself wondering if he had spent some time convalescing as a child.

He argued almost incessantly with our host about mass and inertia and headings and all manner of navigational terms. He was a boorish man, a prig and a bore, but I got the impression from the start that he was also the kind of man that you wanted near if things went wrong. On this expedition it seemed likely that things would go wrong often and with that in mind I choose to endear myself to the man.

There were others with us on the tour, some faces I remember vaguely while others I am utterly unable to forget. Along with Foley there were eight whose names and visages I will take with me to my grave, but there on the first day only Foley and one other stood out. His name was Tommy Vines and he was the strongest man I have ever met.

I'd been aware of him from the start of the tour. He was a huge man, a comedic creation of circus strongman and grizzly bear. He was unkempt as we traversed the corridors of the gondola and reeked a little of sweat and blood. He remained at the back of Ms Thorn's entourage as if affording the shorter men a better view. It was perhaps this trait that made me think of him as a considerate sort. History would see me right on the matter.

I've always had the gift of telling a figure's height, no matter the distance. I would have comfortably put him at six foot five maybe even six. He sported a full beard and long locks on that first occasion, although like the rest of us it wasn't long before MOID had him shorn to tash and crew cut, but there in the fantastic cabins of *The Red Queen*, he was the image of a great mountain bear. I remember thinking I wouldn't have liked to go more than two rounds with the man and instinctively stealing a glance at his hands. They were suitably enormous, and I remember standing there wondering how much of my face one of them would be able to pummel if he decided to swing me a jab. There were other faces, that I would later put to names but only Foley and Vines truly made first impressions.

If you'd told me only one of those two would live to stand on the red planet, I'd have believed you even less than if you'd told me any of us would make it.

The briefing was another blur, my only defence for my indifference was that I was so unconvinced by the whole endeavour that I completely failed to register anything important about it.

We'd been drugged, she told us, and I have to believe that some of the haze surrounding my lapses was due to that.

The drugs felt like being buried alive, that much I can tell you. I have no idea what was in the needle they stuck me with, or the vials they sent us up with, but it was a very peculiar experience. As I said, it felt very much like someone was filling in the world around me, but oddly this brought on a strangely joyous feeling. I wasn't in the least bit concerned about the fact that the world was closing in. Doctor Bill would later describe the experience as a feeling akin to returning to the womb and I could see some sense in his definition.

One by one Ms Thorn jabbed us and eased us into the cockpit of *The Red Queen's* gondola. This seemed to take forever. This moment would become my last memory of Miss Thorn. I constantly tell myself that if I had known, I would have chosen to leave under different circumstances. My body felt limper than my leg after two days in a fever hammock and I couldn't move an inch. It was all I could do to keep my eyes open as the men from the MOID strapped us in and ticked us off their red tape.

After a short spell of eternity, the rumbling began and my skull began to feel like it was trying to escape from my body. Foley had warned us about this.

"We'll all feel the last twangs of gravity as the gondola begins to take up the slack," he said, as our party reached the cockpit for the first time and saw the chairs we'd be strapped into. "But don't worry boys, the effects won't last and as soon as we're free of the Earth you'll feel like you're falling, except there'll be nothing below you, kind of like flying."

I remember I didn't much like the idea of flying and a flashback of *The Carpathian* shook me back into my situation.

I could barely think, but the stress of my head seemed to have subsided and a feeling like a puff on the poppy pipe took over. I remember thinking that I could get used to it.

I don't know how long the numbness lasted. Doctor Bill told me it was nearly a year, but despite everything that happened I simply can't believe that.

The saddest truth was I was so hopelessly disinterested in what I was still convinced was an elaborate jape that I ignored almost everything Ms Thorn had told me.

You'd think some part of me would have made sure that I kept some memories of the means by which I left the very planet I had become so bored with, but sadly not.

I have tried so many times to reconjure the incredible feeling that overcame me as Heather Rose Thorn threw open the heavy velvet drapes and I realised for the first time that we had actually entered the realms of the astrologers.

Jones, Smith, Boyd, Cole, Foley, McCabe, Little Nick, Dr. Jones and Tommy, dear Tommy...

I say their names, so they still matter and take some solace in the hope I am still human.

Death was with us before we left, it was almost as if our enemy lacked patience.

I don't pretend that I will find redemption, only that I may find peace before my final failing...

...No more will come...at least none sent by my hand...

Jones was the first to go. The night can be a lonely place and this night was as much a passing of time, as a place. A cold and terrible place without the glimmer of end.

Fate had seen to it that I was the first through the airtight lock which Jones had used to conceal his crime and his shame. I had barely spoken to Boyd, so it was a surprise to find myself so overcome when I discovered his soiled corpse still clinging to the wheel of the lock.

Jones had stabbed him over a hundred times, but he had gotten off lightly compared to Smith.

In my time in India I'd witnessed such horror and atrocity to turn one to or from religion depending on where one stood at the start, but never could I have imagined such darkness here in the very heavens.

So much blood! So many shades, the first wisps, now brown and terracotta from the slashes on his bound wrists. The darker stains were almost black near his kidneys from where Jones had tried to remove his liver. I tried to fight the urge to turn but failed. My curiosity has never been easily sated, but I garnered no pleasure in the sight of Jones's ruby stained mouth and his teeth still clinging gleefully to a coujon of Smith's liver. I had found the journey unsettling, we all had, but I could not make whatever leap Jones had. I was spared whatever reasoning he might have used to attempt to rationalise this sadism and madness.

We were all weary from fatigue and woozy from the drugs. So, after the gruesome discovery we sealed the compartments where Jones had committed such vile murder and returned to our slumber.

I've seen too much horror in my life. I'd have said that before we left. From the evil that war brings out in us, to the horrifying slow deaths I witnessed in aftermath of the fall of *The Carpathian*. But what Jones did in the hours before our final approach I can barely begin to think about. I had to try to block out the screams and the smell and ultimately everything I saw, just to keep me sane as the gondola made its descent. Foley was at the helm so to speak, although it was unlike any helm I'd ever seen. He insisted we all strapped in, and I couldn't help but stare at the three empty seats opposite me as Foley threw switch after switch.

We were all there in the cockpit as the feeling of mass hit us again. Cole seemed more agitated than usual and one must remember these were far from normal times. He undid his harness and made to leave his seat. I tried to protest, but Foley stole the words from me.

"Cole, return to your seat immediately," he said in a voice of clear authority.

Had I not been so bloody scared I would have been impressed. Cole paid the man no heed and was already at the cockpit bulkhead. I could see Foley toing and froing with the idea of giving chase, but he seemed too intent on his dials and switches. I scanned the cockpit to see who else might take up the pursuit. McCabe was still incoherent and could barely sit upright. Tommy Vines clearly had the intention of assisting, but was finding no purchase with his own harness. Doctor Bill was still unconscious and to his shame Little Nick was pretending to be asleep. Cursing the coward under my breath, I relaxed the clasp on my own harness and tried to stand. As I made it to my feet the cockpit turned the colour of sunset and the stress returned to the base of my skull.

I heard Foley mutter something and it took me a moment to decipher what he had said

"We're breaching the Martian atmosphere," he said, "Please return to your seat Colonel, there's nothing you can do for Cole."

"I'll not let him die now," I said, raising my voice over the rising roar of the engulfing flames. Cole had sealed the bulkhead door and I peered hard into the tiny window. I could see him unscrewing the door to his own cabin as I fought to open the cockpit door. I had nearly succeeded when Cole's own door opened first and he was engulfed in flames from within. I must have been seconds from freeing the main bulkhead door when Foley threw himself at me.

"You'll kill us all man," he said, his voice almost inaudible over the outside din, but I could tell he was screaming. "The cabins aren't built for the pressure, that's why the cockpit has an iron bulkhead door. If you open this door we'll all be killed."

I paused for a second and the gesture probably saved my life, but I was damned if I was going to let Cole go so easily. My hand let go of the bulkhead door and without even a glance I plunged it through the breakaway glass compartment to the left of the door, where the extinguisher was kept. As my hand grasped the cold iron cylinder, I knew Cole was doomed. The weight of the device betrayed its failings, the extinguisher was empty, and I had run out of plans.

Foley dragged me from the window and I was spared the sight of my colleague being roasted alive. The roar of atmospheric entry similarly spared us all from his screams. Foley shoved me back to my seat and then returned to his bank of switches. The feeling in my head was horrendous. I realised I was still clutching the defunct extinguisher and thought about dropping it, but something stopped me. I don't know if perhaps one of Foley's endless sermons on inertia, vectors or velocity had somehow clung to the back of my mind, but I like to think so. So, with the iron cylinder still in my grip I fought to refasten my harness.

The cockpit had already begun to spin and that horrid feeling of nausea I'd experienced right back at the start of the journey came back to me. I fought hard to keep the contents of my stomach where they belonged. Little Nick had given up the charade and was literally screaming as the gondola dropped like lead shot through the red Martian sky. The Doc was still out and McCabe made no suggestion he was even on the same journey as the rest of us.

Tommy Vines said nothing, as usual, and stared hard at some imaginary horizon on the wall opposite. I tried to do the same, but I couldn't take my eyes of Foley. He was still at the controls.

"Get to your seat man," I yelled at him. "We're in the hands of God now."

"No Colonel," he replied with a straight face and firm jaw. "We're still in my hands and be glad for it. I could never trust a god that could make a mistake as great as the human race."

"Damn you man!" I roared over the din of flames. "Strap yourself in or you'll be able to tell god personally what you think of him in about five minutes."

"Nearly there," he said; and I allowed myself a moment of hope.

A second later he made for an empty seat. It wasn't his seat, but the time for choosing was past and I would have done the same. The forces in the cabin were on the very precipice of bearable and I couldn't be sure of anything except the pain in my skull, as we spun like a dervish over the alien landscape. I couldn't tell you in honesty whether the visions I can recall of the descent were flashes from the cockpit window or pure make believe, but they looked spectacular nonetheless.

Then I saw it…

Foley's harness had failed. The man was clinging to his seat with all the might he could muster. My heart stopped. I could barely control my limbs and keep conscious and my harness was intact. I knew the second I saw him struggling to keep his seat that he was dead. Not there in the moment, but soon and without salvation. My heart knew that somewhere in the darkness of the next few moments my friend's strength would fail and he would be thrown around the cockpit like a handkerchief in a gale. The nearest seat with a harness was an impossible fifty feet from him and the nearest occupied seat was mine. He was going to die and he knew it, but with strength I had come to know well in the brief time I had known him, he gave the short time he had left to the rest of us. Throwing his ruined harness to one side, Foley used the rivets of the cockpit itself as hand holds as he navigated the circular room. The noise was deafening and despite my best efforts I was unable to make out what he was obviously trying to shout. He was about halfway across the cockpit when I heard Tommy vines speak.

"Foley says you have to look after the book." He roared at me.

"You can hear him?" I asked. Vine's seat was further from Foley than mine and I could scarcely believe his hearing was better.

196

"I can read his lips. He says he's bringing the book of power to you."

That was the first time I saw the book. Foley had it over his shoulder in its strange black satchel. He was clambering across the cockpit to pass me his burden, but fate was not making death easy for him. I have no name for the forces at play as we plummeted through the Martian atmosphere, but I felt like my body might fail at any second and the whole nightmare journey would come crashing to a halt. I remember thinking that perhaps that wouldn't be such a bad thing.

Foley was at arm's length now, but everything was spinning on some inconceivable axis. I looked around me; the doctor, McCabe and little Nick had all passed out, and only Vines, Foley, and I were conscious as the great rockets finally fired.

These were the boosters that would guide us in and were supposed to take us back. The sound of the rockets brought me back to life and with them came a familiar feeling: Hope. I looked at Foley then with my hopeful eyes, but faith failed me as I focussed. Sure, the rockets would eventually break our fall, but Foley had told me they would fire in stages. This then was only the first phase and Foley had no strength. With his last reserves, he thrust the book into my hands and let go. For a second he seemed to float in front of my face and then the Martian gravity took him, and I closed my eyes. Mercifully I passed out then, although I suspect Tommy vines was not so fortunate. I never asked him if he witnessed Foley's death and he never volunteered, but Vines never struck me as one to look away from anything. Perhaps the great Welshman did see the gruesome sight of our friend and colleague threshed around the cockpit like a calf leg in a mincer, but even if he had, I doubt it would have been worse than the images my own mind conjured after I awoke and saw what the fall had done to him

The Doctor threw up, as he came round and saw the state of the cockpit. Little Nick cried like a girl. McCabe kept his colour and Tommy Vines didn't so much as blink.

Ten of us had set out for the surface of Mars, which only five of us lived long enough to stand upon and all the while I heard that voice it said come, come to me my love.

I rallied the party as soon as we'd stopped moving and shuffled the remainder of the mission into *The Red Queen's* observation lounge. It was dark outside. I hadn't anticipated this and I must have looked surprised because McCabe answered the question I had been forming in my mind.

 "You've been out for about four hours," he said. "It was light when we landed, but there was a dust storm so we couldn't see anything."

"Dust," I said, "that was the one thing I was expecting. Has anyone seen to Cole?" This time it was Tommy that answered.

"There's not much left." He was trying to get into his second lungs when the fire started and roasted him good and proper, lost his lungs too."

"They're made of iron," I said.

"And full of oxygen," Tommy replied. "We're lucky he didn't burn a hole in the hull."

"How many lungs do we have left?" I asked as a sense of panic ran up my backbone.

"We only lost one and there are only five of us left," Vines pointed out. "It will be a while before we worry about breathing."

We wasted no time in strapping on the remaining lungs and Tommy and I each slung a spare.

By the time we'd prepped for a sortie, dawn was breaking over the surface of Mars.

I have never since seen a sunrise like it, nor do I suspect will I ever again. The sky began dark terracotta and slowly shifted through the entire spectrum of red. I saw shades of red I'd never conceived of before, scarlets, bright and vivid like freshly drawn blood, crimsons, lush and luxurious like fine theatre curtains. From pale amber to rust brown, that morning I saw more reds than I thought could exist.

As we disembarked and climbed down the iron ladders below *The Red Queen's* cockpit, the sky continued its journey through the world of red. The suits and lungs did well to insulate us from the cold and acrid atmosphere. As we crept out onto the surface, I made an involuntary gasp as I realised a single tear in the suit would mean my brutal end and Mars would forever be my tomb.

I still have difficulty remembering everything about my journey and I often wonder whether perhaps it was some sort of dream, but then I hear her voice and I remember the moments I could never forget nor conjure.

I had heard it subconsciously from the start. I think it was always there lingering in the space between my thoughts. In the quiet moments I could always hear the idea thrumming softly, urging me on towards my fate. But the second I touched the surface of the red planet, I heard it aloud for the first time...and it was clear for the first time that I was not the only one.

Come to me my love

As the voice spoke, we all reacted, and I knew for the first time since I'd met Ms Thorn that our fates had all been connected. It was the doc that spoke first.

"You all heard that?"

"I suspect we have heard it for some time." I added and a round of nods confirmed my suspicions. We were all destined to be here. It seemed like destiny was closer than ever.

"We should bury the dead." Tommy Vines added and more nods followed.

Angered by his cowardice during the landing I made sure McCabe drew the short straw and was sent to retrieve the bodies of Jones and his meals.

It seemed fitting that I retrieved what I could of Foley. Mercifully I was joined by the doc and the pair of us set to work. The suit's heavy rubber gloves helped a great deal when it came to the gruesome chore, but I still winced occasionally when I came across a flap of skin I recognised; or an organ. I could still hear the voice deep in the back of my head urging us onwards as I worked.

It took less than an hour all in, to pile the remains of our colleagues in a heap on the red Martian soil. The crimson earth, how ironic that name, had the texture of sand, but felt strangely heavy like iron filings.

Vines dug a trench with a fragment of entry debris. No one seemed sure what to do as he piled the corpses into the hole, but McCabe took up a chorus of 'God Save the Queen'. Lacking a reason not to, it wasn't long before we were all singing.

We buried our dead and sang 'God Save the Queen'…

The sheer number of unforgettable sights I witnessed on the journey will never seem rational, but if there was a singular most memorable moment, then perhaps the view that greeted us as we crested the valley ridge could be a contender.

I'd expected rocks, I had expected dust to be honest, I hadn't expected much, but I never imagined that I would see a scarlet palace on a crimson sea.

There below me, was a scene from a daydream. I looked at the doc and he pointed out and low over the ruby waters.

 "Methane," he said surveying the shores of the liquid gas lake. I tried not to think about the extreme conditions required to create such a natural wonder and not for the first time I checked the seals on my suit.

As we crested the lip of our little crater, we could see the palace. Here, half a million miles away from London Town and my common sense, was a great big bloody Martian castle, skirted by a ruby moat of liquid methane.

As we approached from the southern shore we crossed a rusty drawbridge over a ruby moat.

The lake was something, but to be blunt, it paled by comparison to the castle. In my career as a soldier I have come across many castles and they always seem to fall into one of two categories, keeping the enemy out or inspiring fairy tales. The castle that lay before us was truly the first that I would have described as both.

Our mission had one clear outcome and if we were to do our job then all our answers lay in the palace ahead. It was vast almost cityesque in stature and centred around an immense spire which threatened the very heavens with its stiletto summit. The whole building was in immaculate condition, as if the architect had handed it over the day before yesterday. As we entered the strange stone castle it was clear it was deserted.

I raised my hand over my head and the others filed in behind me and together we snaked through courtyard after courtyard.

Come to Me My Love

Strange is a word I realise I am in danger of overusing, but there was no other way to describe the eerie feeling as we surveyed the palace.

Tommy Vines spoke for the first time since I'd watched him bury our dead.

"The place is deserted we should leave before we fall foul of the same curse"

"Tommy," I said, "we're on for the final push. Would you turn back without reaching the summit? No, we have to push on. Something built this place and I for one would know what."

Come to Me My Love

 "So, we can all hear the voice." I said, "Whatever it is, we know we are not alone. This fortress may look defenceless, but clearly there's someone here."

As we progressed through the complex, a singular thought kept nudging me. The stronghold was obviously built to last, but in my years of service I knew there was something wrong about it. It was then that I revised my earlier conclusion. This keep was unholdable, and to my knowledge there was only one reason to build a stronghold one couldn't defend...perhaps two.

"It's a tomb," Tommy said stealing one of my trains of thought.

"Or a prison," I said, unveiling the other.

"Let's hope someone didn't build it for us." Tommy said.

"I don't think I'll ever be that important." I replied.

Somewhere in the corner of conscious I found myself back within the cold granite walls of Bedlam.

I tried and failed to retrace the mental steps back to Mars.

I could sense the clouds on the periphery forming a deep fog bank, and for the moment a sliver of doubt crept over me. It was then that I realised that I was in the presence of Dietmar, or Nurse D. Bloech as I should really call her.

"Back in the land of the living I see." she said with a narrow smile.

She was not an unattractive woman, striking and quick witted. I found myself tracing her stockinged calf idly. She caught my gaze as it met the hem of her pencil skirt and frowned disapprovingly.

I shrugged unabashedly, but truth be told I did feel a little ashamed.

"I did some research," she hinted.

"Oh..."

"These men you mentioned. You said they were part of some Imperial Ministry?"

"MOID..."

"I have been able to locate some of those mentioned in your statement."

Her statement was a sucker punch and I recoiled an inch as if it had been a punch she'd thrown.

"You found them? You found Tommy?"

"I have found a Tommy Vines, but he is not the man you describe...or rather he is not the soldier you described."

"What do you mean?"

"You claimed Tommy had served in The Welsh Guard. That he was a soldier."

"Ten years, from the brief time I served with him, I'd say he was one of the best officers I have ever met."

"That's the problem, this Tommy Vines has never served in the military."

"So, I'm a lunatic and I am where I belong. I bit Carruthers; they're going to lobotomise me."

"Not on my watch."

"Nurse Bloech, why do you choose to torment me? You spent the best part of a year convincing me of my madness and now that finally I am to be free of my insanity, you choose to champion my theories"

"Come to me...come to me my love...what do those words mean to you again? You've often cited them?"

Her manner shifted; this was something new. I sat forward to better mark her expression.

The meander through the crimson halls was a sleepwalk. My mind had wandered so far from the muddied grass that I couldn't tell you anything about the journey. All the while the migraine voice thundered around my skull and I all I could think about was love horrible, horrible love.

The throne room could not have been anything else. The walls were the red of nightmares and madness. A colour I cannot describe with any words I know. It was the colour of rage, the colour of hell. All rationale I had, I left at the door of the great throne room and as I passed through the portal all the humanity drained from me like the blood from a damsel's face seconds before her swoon.

And there on a throne of souls was the Martian Queen in a robe of bones.

I saw myself approach the great chair as if I were watching some cheap actor playing me in some pantomime farce. She was enormous, not vast like a buffalo, but tall like an oak tree. She was the colour of fire, seemingly shifting like flames as I stared at her. Her face was starkly beautiful, the way cliff faces are beautiful, and she wore make up in a fashion I would have imagined Cleopatra to wear. Her eyes were the single most important thing I had ever seen and once I had found their focus, I could not escape them

Once I again I found myself outside my body, as if I were peering in at the room from a grubby window. Then my perspective shifted again and I could see the room and I could see the throne and her eyes. Slowly her eyes began to become the room and then the throne and then I heard the voices of the souls.

I could see the souls and I could hear them, there were so many and their roar was deafening, countless entities raging in the vortex that was at once the Queen's throne and her eyes, they were one and infinite and they were fragile and terrible, but even above their cacophony was her voice, if voice was the word, she spoke, if she were speaking and the words were not words but commands and she commanded me and I could not look at her, nor could I breath, I was faint and fragile just like the voices in the vortex and she reigned over them like a hurricane and she was terrible and her commands were everything and I could do nothing, nothing, nothing, but obey, a voice in my head said strangle McCabe and I saw her smile as I turned to my friend and as I reached out to grab his neck

I saw Tommy Vines do the same to Nick, Old Doctor Bill tried to escape but the Martian Queen she wasn't finished yet, my friend faded and he turned blue, I turn round to see that Tommy finished too, the Martian Queen had given old Bill a knife and in return for that he'd given her his own life, in the end there was just Tommy and I and we both knew that one us had to die and I knew then it could not be me because only the winner gets the Martian Queen and I have never wanted anything more…

I do not know where I found the machete. I can only assume that she had given it to me. It's purpose was clear enough though and for a blizzard moment, I fought my good friend and colleague with tempered steel, countless miles from home on the shores of another world for a demon woman I had never even spoken to. I killed him quickly, he was a strong man, but it seemed to me that her hold on him was not as great as her hold on me and the conflict in him dulled his actions. It is with a little mercy perhaps, that I remember little about our duel other than the outcome for I do not like to entertain the thought that he suffered at my hands, although logic tells me that he most assuredly did. As I knelt to face her with Tommy's head on my lap she laughed, she smiled and then she clapped. It was all that I could ever hoped, but then she opened her scarlet lips and spoke she said.

"Your planet had nothing to fear, for I am just a prisoner here. I can never leave these four walls let alone launch an assault, but I greatly admire your desires and by feeding on them I survive and you've sent enough here to me to last at least a hundred years. But a girl's got to eat and soon I'll be needing fresher meat, so I'm sending you on home, so you can tell others to come. Come To Me My Love…"

That's the last I saw of the Red Queen or the Red planet or any of them… You'll think I'm mad, but be careful not to dig to deep. Dietmar did and Dietmar believes me. I know what you're going to say, I've heard it so many times. There are no Spirit Guns, or great Iron Gondolas, Delft is just a town and the Carpathians mere mountains, there are no Zeppelins anymore and there never was a MOID or a Heather Rose Thorn and you know what? You would be right. But I did not come from this world and in my world we heard the red queen's call and we answered. In this world I can still hear her calling. She feeds on our sense of adventure, a great vampiric entity out there on the cold red rocks of Mars. She calls and we answer, and I know it happened because I still have the book. The power book, the one that sent us to Mars in the first place, the beautiful and deadly book that offered us all the answers. I still have it and it still has a little charge and later today I'm going to open up the power book and let Dietmar look through its little glass window and then I'm going to take the little capsule Miss Thorn gave me in case anything went wrong. Maybe in this world you can kill her and ring some vengeance from her great red halls for the friends and colleagues that I lost. I want to smash the book and prevent

Dietmar from using its vile power to launch a similar assault, but I can't... because she calls still and I still love her.

THE END

ABOUT THE AUTHOR

Neil Campbell is a published songwriter, award-winning screenwriter and fledgling novelist. Neil credits ADHD, which was diagnosed late in his life, for the adventures, mishaps and creativity which has plagued and blessed his ridiculous life in equal measures. As the founder member and main songwriter, it's safe to say The Dark Design is all his fault. He lives in Brighton, collects hopeless causes and has a magic dog (seriously Google Captain the Magic schnauzer).

Do not fear the tales you read,
Or the sights that you have seen.
Remember what old Bill said,
"It was only just a dream."

ACCREDITATION IMAGES

Page 3 Image of Professor Elemental - Mangaka Maiden Photography 2020 (CC-by-20)

Page 6 image provided by The Dark Design

Page 8 image provided by The Dark Design

Page 10 image provided by The Dark Design

Page 18 Tom Bones Comic. Graves Bernd Thaller (CC-by-20). Skull Grave Andrew Malone (CC-by-20).

Page 19 Tom Bones Comic. Widow Hillary Robinson by Nils Visser, model Cair Emma Going.

Page 20 Tom Bones Comic. Close-ups face Gypsy Queen Reeda Malik (CC-by-20). Caravan David Koranda (CC-by-20). Graves Bernd Thaller (CC-by-20). Horned Demon Stiller Beobachter (CC-by-20).

Page 21 Tom Bones Comic. Close-up face Gypsy Queen Reeda Malik (CC-by-20). Demon face, Staffan Vilcans, (CC-by-20).

Page 22 image provided by The Dark Design

Page 26 image provided by The Dark Design

Page 27 image provided by The Dark Design

Page 29 title Page SALT. Lian2011 ID 22508839. Image licensed to Cider Brandy Scribblers by Dreamstime.com

Page 33 courtesy of Graphics Fairy

Page 35 courtesy of Graphics Fairy

Page 38 courtesy of Graphics Fairy

Page 39 & 43 Ekaterina Tutynina ID 92175619. Image licensed to Cider Brandy Scribblers by Dreamstime.com

Page 42 author picture LM Cooke provided by author.

Page 46 image provided by The Dark Design

Page 48 image provided by The Dark Design

Page 49 Image of S-78 courtesy of Janneke Stam.

Page 50 image by Bonsart Bokel

Page 70 author image Bonsart Bokel provided by author.

Page 71 image provided by The Dark Design

Page 73 image provided by The Dark Design

Page 76 image by Nils Visser

Page 77 background Nils Visser. Image Duke Box provided by Jack Bicknell.

Page 78 background & gibbet Nils Visser. Image Duke Box provided by Jack Bicknell.

Page 79 background Nils Visser. Pirate Queen Corin Spinks

Page 80 background Nils Visser. Image Duke Box provided by Jack Bicknell.

Page 81 background Nils Visser. Ghost Neil Campbell.

Page 82 background Nils Visser. Image Duke Box provided by Jack Bicknell.

Page 83 background Nils Visser. Image Duke Box provided by Jack Bicknell.

Page 84 background Nils Visser. Image Duke Box provided by Jack Bicknell.

Page 85 image by Corin Spinks, model Lara Blair

Pages 92, 96, 98, 99, 100, 101, 103, 106, 110, 119, 120, 121, 122, 127, 131, 134, 136, 139, 140, 141, 143, 144, 146, 148, 154 images by Yuliya Nazaryan, licensed to Cider Brandy Scribblers by Dreamstime.com

Page 149 photo by Craig Neesam, model Cair Emma Going

Page 150 author image Nils (Nisse) Visser by Corin Spinks.

Page 151 logo Duke Box, copyright Duke Box/Jack Bicknell

Page 156 image provided by The Dark Design

Pages 161, 163, 164, 170, 175, 177, 178, 185, 191, 198, 201, 204, 206, 209 image by Yuliya Nazaryan, licensed to Cider Brandy Scribblers by Dreamstime.com

Page 162 The Red Queen by Laura Norris

Page 205 author image Jeanette Macklin Photography

Page 206 background Nils Visser. Image Duke Box provided by Jack Bicknell.